FIRELORD

Michael Scott

This is for Nicole, who waited very patiently...

FIRELORD
Third of the De Danann Tales

Michael Scott

WOLFHOUND PRESS
IRISH AMERICAN BOOK COMPANY (IABC)

This edition reprinted 1997
First published 1994 by
WOLFHOUND PRESS Ltd
68 Mountjoy Square
Dublin 1

Wolfhound Press receives financial assistance from The Arts Council/ An Chomhairle Ealaíon, Dublin, Ireland.

British Library Cataloguing in Publication Data
Scott, Michael
   Firelord. — (De Danann Tales Series)
   I. Title II. Series
   823.914 [J]

   ISBN 0-86327-385-8

Published in the U.S. and Canada by Irish American Book Company (IABC)
6309 Monarch Park Place, Niwot, Colorado 80503
Phone 303 530 1352 Fax 303 530 4488

Cover design and illustration: Peter Haigh
Map: Aileen Caffrey
Typesetting: Wolfhound Press
Printed in Great Britain by Cox & Wyman Ltd., Reading, Berkshire.

Contents

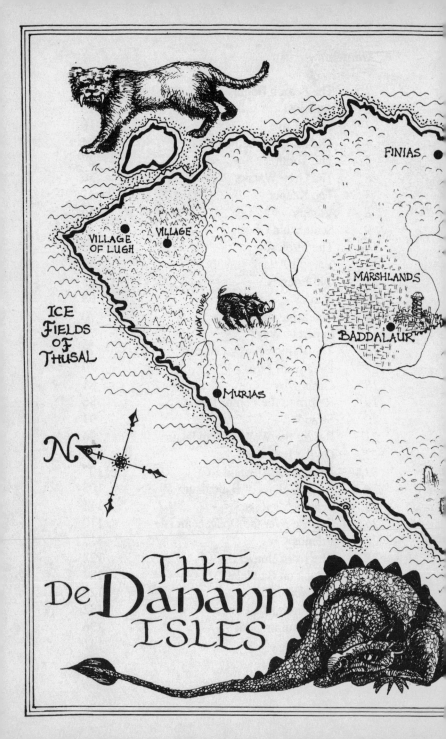

FINIAS

VILLAGE OF LUGH

VILLAGE

MARSHLANDS

ICE FIELDS OF THUSAL

MIDA RIVER

BADDALAUR

MURIAS

N

THE De Danann ISLES

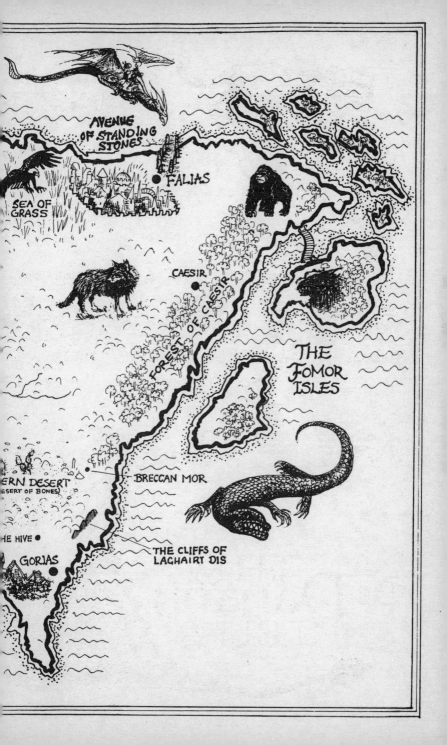

Paedur the Bard spread the enormous chart across the table. Tiny flakes of parchment broke away and crumbled onto the floor. The bard dropped heavy wooden-bound books onto two of the corners, while he weighted down another corner with his knife.

'Come and have a look at this,' he said quietly, glancing over his shoulder, his dark eyes large and liquid in his long narrow face. Pulling strands of long black hair out of his eyes, he tapped the chart with the flat metal hook that took the place of his left hand. The metal rang with a dull chime.

'Ally, this is the De Danann Isle,' he said to the young woman standing beside him. 'Your brother could be anywhere on it.' He touched a red dot almost in the centre of the map. 'We are here in Baddalaur.'

Ally leaned over the map, reading the symbols, guessing which ones meant mountains and rivers, marshes and deserts. 'I never realised the island was so big,' she murmured.

Paedur pointed to the left hand side of the map. 'The De Danann Isle fills the sea from the Land of the Toltecs, the copper-skinned folk, to the Land of the Dark Folk here in the east.'

'From South America to Africa,' Ally whispered. She looked at Paedur. 'In my time those lands have different names. This sea here is called the Atlantic Ocean ... and the De Danann Isle will be called Atlantis. In my time Atlantis is a myth, a legend.'

Paedur's thin lips curled in a smile. 'And yet you are here.'

Ally nodded, looking at the chart again. Six months ago — was it only six months? — she and her brother Ken had been pulled back to the De Danann Isle by rogue magic. There they had met the young bard, Paedur and joined with him and his companions, Faolan the Windlord, Megan the Warrior Maid and Ragallach, the Torc Allta were-beast, in their battle against the evil Emperor, Balor. When they defeated Balor, the Windlord had used his magic to send them forward to their own time, but the Emperor had sent one of his deadly lizard-like Fomor warriors after them. The beast had nearly killed them. As the enormous lizard loomed over them with his stone sword raised high, Ken and Ally had used the magical amulets the Windlord had given them to slip back in time to the De Danann Isle and rejoin their companions. The days that followed had been terrifying, but, with the aid of the Earthlord, they had managed to defeat Balor once again and destroyed his palace. Ken and Ally had returned to their own time ... but they had only been back for a few minutes when Ken vanished before his sister's eyes. Ally had immediately used the magical amulet to return to the De Danann Isle to search for her brother.

The girl shook her head, the soft light from the oil-lamps running copper and gold from her bright red hair. 'He could be anywhere,' she whispered. She could feel her throat begin to burn and tears stung her eyes. 'I'll never find him.'

Paedur reached out and squeezed Ally's shoulder. 'We will find him,' he said simply.

'How?'

'Magic.' He held out his right hand. 'Put both your hands in mine,' he said. She extended her hands immediately, her flesh pale against Paedur's deeply tanned skin. The bard stretched out his left arm with the flat of the metal hook just above the surface of the chart. 'Now I want you to visualise your brother,' he said quietly. 'Relax. Let your mind go blank. Now, think about Ken. See him in your head. Talk to him.'

Closing her eyes, Ally breathed deeply and concentrated on her brother. Although he was a month and a year younger than her, they were alike enough to be taken for twins occasionally. He would be fourteen soon, tall, skinny, bright red hair tumbling over his pale green eyes. He drove her mad and they fought constantly, but the last time, when they had been on the De Danann Isle and Ken had been badly injured, she had realised just how much she loved him. She tried hard to remember every detail of his face, but she found it easier to remember his expressions: his face smooth and innocent as he waited for her to discover the spider in her bed or that he'd superglued her bedroom door closed, or he'd hidden the door to her wardrobe. And then she remembered the look in his eyes when he'd held onto her with every last ounce of strength as she dangled over the edge of the abyss on the Fomor Isle.

'Ken ...' she whispered. She could see him laughing, the look of delight in his eyes when he'd got the computer he'd wanted for Christmas, the look of terror in his eyes in the moments before he'd vanished, less than a dozen heartbeats after they'd returned to their own time. 'Ken ... Where are you, Ken?'

Paedur moved his hook over the map of the ancient island. His eyes were closed, his forehead creased in concentration, strong white teeth biting into his lower lip. Starting in the Northlands, he slowly moved his hook from left to right, came down, then shifted it right to left, covering the entire map in long smooth strokes. Ally's hands were moist in his, and he could feel her shaking with the effort of concentrating on her brother. The sound of her voice calling her brother's name was the only noise in the room.

A tingle in his arm alerted him and his eyes snapped open.

The tiny lines of script etched into the metal of his hook were glittering softly. Paedur moved his arm from side to side, watching as the lights died, then burned brighter when he moved his arm back again.

'Now Ally,' Paedur said insistently. 'We're close now. So close. Concentrate hard.'

The girl's grip tightened painfully on the bard's hand, her fingernails digging into his flesh. She could see her brother clearly in her head now. His hair was wild, his head bowed ...

and then he slowly raised his head and opened his eyes.

Hot wind ...

Sand ...

The smell of burning in the air ...

The sudden images were so clear that Ally blinked her eyes open, and the image faded. 'I saw him,' she whispered, abruptly terrified. 'And I felt hot wind on my face, and there was sand beneath my hands, and I could smell something bitter burning.' She looked at Paedur in astonishment. 'It was so real. It was almost as if I was there.'

The bard nodded. 'It was real. Look.' He lifted his left arm, and then slowly allowed his hook to approach the map. When it was just above the surface of the ancient chart, the lines of script in the metal began to sparkle, then glow, until suddenly they were burning with a cold grey light. Paedur lifted his arm and pointed to a spot on the map, to the west and south of Baddalaur. 'Ken is here, in the Western Desert — the Desert of Bones.'

If the assassin ever had a name, he had long ago forgotten it. He was known simply as Blade, because he carried dozens of blades around his body ... and because he liked to do his work with a knife. There was a knife in his hand now as he moved stealthily down the empty corridors of the great College of Baddalaur, his soft-soled sandals making no sound on the stone floor, his black and grey clothing blending into the shadows.

Blade paused as the corridor divided. He had memorised a map of his route and knew that the left hand corridor led up to the library archives, while the right led down into the classrooms.

Blade moved to the left.

His heart was pounding in his chest, but with excitement, not fear and he was aware of the fluttering in the pit of his stomach. He knew the feeling and welcomed it. The nervousness would keep him alert. He touched the flat knife strapped to his arm beneath his sleeve, the polished metal cool against his skin. There was a second knife tucked into his belt, and he wore a third on a cord around his neck. Flat throwing knives and razor sharp throwing stars were woven into his belt.

Blade didn't know who had hired him. The innkeeper at the Crossed Swords Inn had given him a polished wooden tube sealed at both ends with wax. Blade's name had been burnt into the wood. Within the tube, Blade had found the names of two of his three victims wrapped around a finger-length of solid gold.

Blade weighed the little stick of gold in his hand, expertly gauging its value at around two thousand gold pieces. Blade's usual fee was one hundred pieces. Unfolding the scrap of parchment, he carefully spelled out the names of his victims: Paedur the Bard and the red-haired human female with the strange name: Ally. Blade knew that she was sister to a red-haired human who travelled with her, but he hadn't been seen around Baddalaur. The assassin had looked at the scrap of paper for a long time. He knew now why he had been offered twenty times his usual price. These two — the bard and the red-haired girl — along with some others of around their own age had defeated the Emperor Balor on two occasions. But the Emperor had made the mistake of underestimating them; Blade would not make the same mistake.

He had taken days to prepare for this job, carefully scouting out the College, watching his victims, noting their movements, memorising the layout of the floors. This was going to be his last job. After tonight, he was going to retire, and maybe open up an inn or a small martial arts school.

The assassin stopped at the top of the stairs. He knew that his victims had their bed chambers on this floor. Holding the black-bladed knife flat against his leg, Blade moved towards the first door.

The assassin's teeth flashed in a quick smile. One of his spies in the college had supplied him with a detailed floor plan, and he knew that the first door at the top of the stairs was the girl's bedroom. The door wasn't locked. Sliding into the room, he allowed the door to close behind him, then he waited a few moments until his eyes adjusted to the dim light.

The room was empty except for a simple wooden table holding a basin of water, and a low narrow bed in the corner. A bundled shape sprawled across the bed, snoring gently. Holding the knife tightly in his left hand, Blade crept closer to the bed.

This was going to be easy.

Catching hold of the rough blanket between thumb and forefinger, Blade suddenly twitched it away. The figure on the bed rolled over as he raised his knife. Its head moved ... and Blade suddenly found he was looking into the face of a nightmare, blazing pink eyes above curving white tusks.

With a high-pitched squealing grunt a beast reared up, white tusks flashing, razor sharp teeth closing around the assassin's wrist.

With a yelp of pain, Blade dropped his knife and struck out at the creature, feeling a smooth body beneath rough hairy skin. It was a pig! No, not a pig — a boar. He struck the creature again and it released his hand as it tumbled onto the bed, still squealing. As Blade scrabbled for another knife, the creature launched itself at his chest, hooves tearing at his skin, teeth clicking before his nose, its breath warm and moist against his lips. Dropping the knife, Blade caught the boar in both hands and flung it away from him. It struck the wall with a sickening thump and went still.

The assassin snatched up his two knives and raced towards the door. There was nothing he could do tonight. The pig's squeals would have wakened the whole college.

The door suddenly swung open, a tall figure filling the opening. Before it could lift the burning torch it held in its right hand, Blade lashed out with his knife — but it struck metal, sparks dancing in the light, briefly illuminating a curved silver hook that took the place of the figure's left hand.

The shadowy figure lifted the torch and yellow light flowed down the young bard's thin face.

Blade struck at him again, and this time Paedur used the burning torch to fend off the attack, sparks spilling across the assassin's black leather jerkin.

Without turning around, Paedur said, 'Ally, get the guards — now! I'll hold him here.'

Blade caught a glimpse of bright red hair as the girl he had come to kill raced down the corridor, calling for the guards.

Paedur waved the torch in front of him, keeping the assassin away. 'Who sent you?' he demanded.

'I don't know,' Blade hissed truthfully. He moved the knife in his hand, weaving it to and fro, trying to send a reflection of the torchlight into the young man's eyes, but Paedur kept shifting the torch.

'You are an assassin?' Paedur asked.

'I am Blade.'

'I've heard of you. You're supposed to be the best.'

'I am the best.' He lashed out with the knife, but the bard caught the blade on his hook, twisting it out of the assassin's hand, sending it flying into the wall, where it stuck, point first, vibrating gently. 'There is no way out of this room,' Paedur said softly. 'We're six floors up.' He stopped, hearing shouts behind him. 'And the guards are on their way.'

'I have been hired to kill you,' Blade hissed. 'I have taken my fee, and I will not rest until I have fulfilled my contract.' Then he turned and raced towards the window.

'Stop ...' Paedur began.

Ducking his head, Blade launched himself forward, bursting through the thick window in an explosion of wood and glass.

Paedur raced to the window. He was in time to see the assassin open his arms, his cloak spread wide, a pair of leathery wings snap open to catch the chill night air. In a long slow spiral, the assassin glided downwards.

'Who was it? Where's he gone?' Ally asked, racing back into the room. She followed Paedur's pointing finger, and saw the huge bat-like shape drop onto a rooftop.

'An assassin. Sent to kill one or both of us.'

'But why? Who would send him?' Ally asked. 'Only Balor would want us dead ... and he is dead.'

'Balor was not our only enemy,' Paedur reminded her softly.

~

Blade pulled off his cloak, the bamboo struts tearing into the tough leather material that opened out into the wings. He was trembling in a mixture of rage and fear. He had never once failed on a mission; never before had he run from ... from a one-handed boy! If anyone ever learned of this he would be a laughing stock.

The assassin turned to look up at Baddalaur. Outlined in a high window, tiny figures moved against the light. The bard had humiliated him. Well, the bard had better look out: his days were numbered. Now it was more than a job, it was personal.

~

Paedur pulled the dagger out of the wall and examined it. Ally stood before him, holding the whimpering pink pig in her arms. 'He's bruised all over,' she murmured.

'Ragallach saved our lives,' Paedur said. 'We're lucky he came in here to sleep in your bed. If he hadn't given the alarm, it's unlikely either you or I would have seen the morning. That assassin is one of the best in Baddalaur.'

'Well, we've defeated him. He will not be back.'

'Oh yes he will,' Paedur said grimly. 'He's not going to rest until we're dead. He's been paid to kill us,' he added in a whisper. 'He'll keep coming until he gets us ...'

'Or we get him,' Ally said quietly.

It was hot.

Ken rolled over, feeling sand rub against his cheek, harsh and raw.

The first time he'd woken he'd thought he was having a dream, and he'd drifted back into an uneasy sleep. When he'd woken again and discovered that his surroundings hadn't changed, he'd realised that this was no dream. He was in a small cave, lying on a bed of rough sand. Through the circular opening directly in front of him, he could see a sky that was so pale it looked white, and a distant line of mountains that shimmered in a heat haze.

And it was hot.

Every breath he took dried his mouth, coating his tongue and throat in gritty grains of sand. Beads of sweat popped out on his skin, only to dry off immediately. His head itched unbearably. Even his eyeballs felt dry.

When he eventually crawled to the mouth of the cave and looked out, he discovered it was half way up a sheer cliff ... and there was no way down.

Feeling sick and dizzy, Ken crawled to the back of the cave and curled up into a ball. He would have cried if he could, but he had no moisture for tears. Eventually, he fell into an exhausted sleep.

Ken awoke shivering. It was dark outside and the purple circle of sky through the cave mouth was ablaze with countless stars. Pushing himself up into a sitting position, groaning aloud as cramped arms and legs protested, he discovered a squat stone jug and a carved wooden plate on the ground before him. Too tired to be surprised, he lifted the jug and shook it to and fro. Liquid gurgled inside. He sniffed at the opening, but he couldn't smell anything. Bringing the jug to his mouth, he tilted it back, tasting the liquid with his tongue. It was water. He opened his mouth ... when a shadow shifted on the other side of the cave.

'If you drink too deeply, your stomach will cramp, and you will twist in agony.'

Ken tried to scramble into a standing position, but the cave was too low and he bumped his head on the smooth roof. Gripping tightly to the jug — he could use it as a weapon — he tried to make out the shape in the darkness.

'Who are you?' His voice was thick and slurred, barely above a mumble. Moistening his lips and mouth with the cool water, he tried again, and this time his voice was clearer. 'Who are you?' Then the questions came in a quick tumble. 'Where am I? What am I doing here? Where's Ally, my sister?'

'Sip the water,' the figure said quietly, ignoring the questions, 'take a little of the bread.'

'I want answers,' Ken demanded.

'I have none to give you. Now drink.'

For a brief moment, Ken thought about throwing the jug at the shape and making a dash for the opening. There had to be a ladder or something ...

'The rope was withdrawn when I entered this cave,' the shape said. 'It will only be lowered for me.'

Ken sat down with a bump. Could this figure read his mind?

'I cannot read your mind, but it is not difficult to guess your thoughts or intentions.' The voice was male, Ken guessed, but it was impossible to guess the age. 'You looked at the cave mouth and your grip tightened on the jug — I saw your knuckles whiten.

Then, when I told you what you were thinking, you sat down suddenly, obviously shocked, believing that I could read your thoughts. Am I correct?'

'Yes,' Ken said shortly. The shape in the darkness had made it all sound so simple.

'Now drink — please. Take small sips. Eat a little of the bread. You will find it hard, so moisten it with some of the water. Chew slowly.'

The boy raised the jug to his lips and took a sip. The water was deliciously cool as it slid down his throat. He hiccuped immediately. Breaking off a corner of the bread — it snapped with a sharp crack — he popped a piece into his mouth. It felt like a piece of wood, but when he took another sip of water, it softened and his mouth was flooded with a sweet, spicy taste.

'All I am allowed to tell you is that we mean you no harm,' the shape said quietly.

'Am I on the De Danann Isle?' the boy asked.

'Of course,' the figure said, sounding surprised. 'Where else would you be?'

'Is my sister here?'

'I do not know your sister.'

'She looks a bit like me: red hair, pale skin, freckles.'

'You are the only red-haired human I have ever seen. Now drink, eat. Gather your strength. We have a long way to go before the sun rises.'

Ken sipped the cold water and chewed the bread, thinking furiously. It seemed like only moments ago when he and Ally had returned from the De Danann Isle having defeated Balor. Colum the Earthlord had pulled the Emperor's palace down around him. Then Faolan the Windlord had used his magic to send them forward to their own time once again. He had been standing beside Ally in the ruin of his bedroom, wondering how he was going to explain the mess to his parents, when he'd noticed that the snowflakes whirling in through the shattered window were melting on his skin, the water droplets bubbling and hissing. And then he realised that he felt hot — so hot — even though the room was bitterly cold. He remembered turning, reaching for Ally ... but suddenly she had seemed too far away, and he was falling, falling, falling ...

'Time to go.'

'Do you have a name?' Ken asked. 'I'm Ken.'

The figure paused and seemed to take a long time before responding. 'I had a name once ... Rua, I think it was. Yes, Rua.'

'Are you a warrior, Rua?'

'I am priest!' Rua sounded insulted. Leaning out of the cave mouth, he gave a short sharp whistle. Moments later a thick knotted rope slithered down the cliff face. Rua caught it, and pulled it tight. 'Can you climb?'

'Well ...' Ken said hesitantly. 'I'm afraid of heights.'

'Then don't look down,' the priest said. 'I'll be behind you. If you fall, you'll bring me down with you. And it's a long way down,' he added.

Ken crawled to the mouth of the cave and stared out. The stars were still glittering hard and sharp and bright in the heavens, and red spots of fire winked on the horizon. He looked down, but couldn't see anything, except the vague shape of the rope disappearing into the darkness. Rubbing his sweat-damp hands on the legs of his leather trousers — he was still wearing his De Danann clothes — he reached out and caught the rope.

The climb wasn't as difficult as he'd thought. Loops had been woven into the thick knotted rope and by putting his feet into the loops, he found he could haul himself up easily. He stopped about half way up, shivering as the cold night air chilled the sweat on his body. Standing in the loops, holding tightly to the rope, he looked around.

It was difficult to make out details in the starlight, but now that his eyes had become accustomed to the dim light, he noticed that there were no trees, bushes or grass anywhere. The surrounding countryside seemed to be a flat rocky wasteland, broken occasionally by tall twisting spires of stone, looking black against the purple sky. A single finger of orange-red flame flared from one of the spires. Far off in the distance a creature howled, the mournful sound carried on the wind.

'Hurry,' Rua hissed from below. 'The sun will rise soon.'

'What's the rush?' Ken muttered, pulling himself upwards. He hands were beginning to sting from the rough rope and his shoulder muscles were aching.

'When the sun rises, travel will be impossible,' Rua snapped, moving up behind Ken.

Ken reached the top of the cliff and was groping for a hand-hold when a rasping hiss stopped him. Sand? Wind? Rock scraped, pebbles clicking softly together. He pulled his foot out of the loop and tried to move down, but Rua was too close.

'What's wrong?'

'There's something up here,' Ken whispered. 'Move back.'

'There's nothing ...' Rua began.

A flat triangular-shaped head appeared over the edge of the cliff, waving gently to and fro.

'Sand-eel,' Rua breathed. 'Don't move. Its bite brings lingering agonised death.'

Ken swallowed hard, sour bile at the back of his throat, icy sweat coating his hands. He was terrified of snakes. The sand-eel moved directly above his head. The wind ruffled Ken's hair and the serpent twitched back, forked tongue flickering wildly.

'Don't move,' Rua whispered. 'The eels are blind, but are sensitive to heat and vibrations.'

With his eyes fixed on the serpent, Ken couldn't even nod. Icy sweat was trickling down his forehead, curling off the tip of his nose, gathering on his top lip. He bit the inside of his cheek to prevent himself from sneezing.

The eel's head dipped. Ken stopped breathing.

Infinitely slowly, its dry flesh rasping off the sand-covered stones, the serpent wound its patterned body around the thick rope and began to slither down. Forked tongue flickering, tickling Ken's fingers, moving moistly across his sweat-damp flesh, the eel writhed down the rope.

Gritting his teeth, squeezing his eyes tightly shut, Ken felt the eel slither across his hands, its long, muscular body rippling smoothly. Its head tapped against his chest, tongue dancing madly against his shirt which was now stuck to his flesh with sweat. He was sure it would feel his thumping heart.

The gently bumping head moved around his chest, knocking against his ribs, moving to his side. With a growing sense of horror, Ken realised that the snake was coming off the rope and coiling itself around his body. Panic bubbled up inside him. He knew he couldn't remain on the rope for very much longer, the coarse rope had rubbed the flesh from his hands, leaving them raw and burning and his shoulder muscles were rigid bars of agony.

As the eel's head moved down his spine, its tail came off the rope, suddenly giving Ken an idea just how long it was. It slithered down his thigh and coiled around his leg. When it reached his foot he had the sudden urge to try and kick it off ... but he knew if he did that, then it would only fall onto Rua's head.

Suddenly it was gone from his leg, wrapping itself around the rope again, moving lower, coiling across Rua's hands.

Ken could move now — his every sense was urging him to push upwards, haul himself off the dangling rope, but he didn't move. He remained still, holding the rope tight so that it wouldn't move and the eel wouldn't attack Rua.

It seemed like hours later — though he knew it could only be minutes — before the priest said, 'It's gone.'

As Ken reached over the edge of the cliff, a calloused hand appeared out of the darkness and hauled him upwards, landing him on his feet with a bump. Whirling around, Ken discovered that the cliff top was filled with the dark robed priests. When Rua's hand appeared over the edge, he too was hauled to his feet.

Standing before Ken, he pushed back his hood, revealing an almost skull-like face, the flesh drawn tight over prominent bones, eyes lost in deep shadows. Starlight glistened on the sweat on his bald skull. The priest smiled, a flash of white teeth in the gloom. 'That was a brave thing you did. The goddess chose well when she chose you.'

The were-change came over the creature suddenly, twisting and turning its body, its bones audibly cracking, muscles stretching and popping like creaking leather. When the shuddering stopped, a man-shaped creature lay on the bed where, only moments before, a small pink pig had been lying. The creature sat up with a groan, raising an enormous paw to rub its ribs.

'How do you feel?' Ally asked.

Ragallach na Torc Allta shrugged, then winced as bruised muscles protested. He was a Torc Allta, one of the were-folk; at night he wore the body of a pig, but transformed with the coming of the dawn into the semblance of man. 'I ache everywhere,' he grumbled. His flat snout wrinkled wetly. 'But I have his smell now; I'll know him anywhere.'

'That was very brave of you,' Ally said softly. She ran her hand down Ragallach's arm, feeling his coarse reddish hair rasp beneath her palm. 'He could have killed you.'

The Torc Allta bared his teeth in a terrifying grimace, but Ally had come to recognise it as a smile. 'When I was very young, the shaman of my tribe — what you would call a wise woman — foretold that I would live until the end of the world. I knew I was in no danger.' He raised his great head and looked at the broken window, tusks yellowing in the early morning light. 'What happened to him?'

'He jumped out,' Paedur said, entering the room, balancing a wooden tray precariously with his hook. Sitting down on the edge of the bed, he passed Ally and Ragallach beakers of warm bitter milk. 'He was wearing a contraption of leather wings on a bamboo framework. It wasn't very strong, but then it didn't have to be: it carried him to the nearest rooftop, where he made his escape.'

Ragallach wiped the back of his paw across his mouth, brushing away the droplets of white liquid that clung to his chin. 'Do we have any idea who he was or why he was sent?'

Paedur concentrated on slicing a rough-skinned fruit in three even pieces. Without looking up, he said, 'He was an assassin, and he said his name was Blade. He is notorious in Baddalaur and throughout the De Danann Isles. He is one of the best — and certainly the most expensive — of his type. We don't know who sent him, though you can be sure it was one of Balor's men, but we do know that Ally was certainly his target.' Paedur handed the largest piece of fruit to the Torc Allta, who swallowed it with rind and pips. 'I'm just wondering why he didn't kill you when he had the chance.'

'Ragallach was in his pig shape; maybe this Blade wasn't expecting to find a pig,' Ally suggested.

Paedur nodded. 'That's possible.'

'And I did have my teeth in his wrist at the time,' Ragallach added.

Paedur looked up suddenly, a smile twisting his lips. 'You bit him?'

'On the wrist.' Ragallach's tusks appeared in a quick smile. 'And I scratched his chest with my paws.' He gave an abrupt squeal. 'Of course!'

'Of course? Of course what?' Ally demanded, looking from Ragallach to the young bard. 'What?'

The bard's dark eyes were dancing. 'If Ragallach bit the human, then those wounds will be red and angry this morning.'

'Infection,' Ally said.

'What?'

'Infection. Probably caused by the dirt beneath Ragallach's paws, or microbes on his teeth.'

'Infection?' Paedur stumbled over the unusual word.

'Micro ... microbes?' Ragallach said.

Ally looked at them blankly, suddenly wondering how she was going to explain infection and bacteria in terms they would understand. 'There are creatures so small that you cannot even see them ...' she began, and stopped. 'They live in dirt ...' She stopped again. Both the bard and the Torc Allta were fastidiously clean. 'I'm not saying you are dirty,' she said quickly.

Paedur's smile was gently mocking. 'Perhaps it would be better if you didn't tell us,' he said. 'I'm not sure we want to know.'

'I think you're right,' Ally said gratefully. She bit into the melon-shaped fruit. 'Tell me what's so important about the assassin's injuries?' she asked.

'He has the mark of the beast on him,' the Torc Allta said. 'Unless he has his wounds treated by an expert, then his flesh will swell, he will burn with fever and dream strange and terrifying dreams.'

'What happens then?'

'If he still isn't treated, he will start to become one of the were-folk,' Paedur said. 'The change can drive people mad. If he bites others, then they too will become were-creatures.'

'But surely the assassin will know all this,' Ally said.

The bard nodded. 'He will have to go for treatment.'

'Where?' Ally asked.

Paedur looked at Ragallach. The Torc Allta's tusks flashed in a smile. 'An honest doctor would report the wounds to the authorities ...'

The bard nodded. 'There's only one place he could go.'

~

Blade moved slowly through the quiet morning streets. He kept his right arm hidden beneath his cloak, holding it close to his body. Every movement was agony, and already his wrist had swelled up to almost twice its normal size. He had been marked by the beast and he knew that if he didn't get treatment soon, then he would turn into one of the were-creatures.

This was the oldest part of Baddalaur, the town that had grown up around the ancient College of Bards. The streets were narrow and winding, and the upper floors of the buildings crowded so close together that neighbours could touch hands over the street. The sun never penetrated to street level, and honest citizens rarely came down here. This part of the town belonged to Blade and people like him: criminals, thieves, assassins and mercenaries. However, Blade knew these streets well; an orphan, he had grown up and played in the narrow alleyways, living rough, stealing fruit and bread to survive.

The small assassin stopped in a dark alleyway and looked across an enclosed courtyard. There was a fountain in the centre of the courtyard, but it had long since stopped working and its basin was clogged with rubbish and filth. All that remained of the statue that had once stood over the fountain was a pair of feet. What looked like the dilapidated shells of houses surrounded the courtyard, but Blade knew that appearances were deceptive. Every rotten door was barred with long strips of metal or reinforced wood, and all the lower windows were shuttered and barred.

The house the assassin was looking for was directly across from the opening of the alleyway. It stood slightly taller than the rest, and had once belonged to a famous warrior-bard. The house, and the others in the courtyard were relics of the time when this part of town had been fashionable and not ruled by criminals.

Blade took a deep breath, calming himself. His hand was on fire now, his wrist and elbow throbbing. He wasn't sure how quickly the were-change took hold, but if the disease was carried in the blood then the curse was probably working its way through his body even as he stood there. He had only ever seen one man who had been infected by one of the were-folk. The man — a hill farmer from the Northlands — had been bitten by one of the Madra Allta, the Wolf-Kind, in a fight in an inn. When night fell, he threw off his human form to become a were-wolf, a terrible, terrifying creature driven only by the need to kill. Blade didn't want to become something like that. Once, his proudest boast had been that he feared nothing, but he was terrified now.

Blade looked at the door of the house across the courtyard. The winged crest of a doctor was barely visible beneath the layer of grime. The assassin glanced into the sky, judging the time by the position of the sun and shadows. The doctor's office would open soon. Dule the physician would treat him; Dule treated everyone, regardless of their injury; the aged doctor asked no questions and only accepted payment from those who could afford to pay.

Blade used his left hand to lift his right arm out from beneath his cloak. The swelling stretched from his fingertips to his elbow, and his skin had turned dark red, almost purple.

He couldn't wait!

Covering his arm with his cloak, Blade looked around making sure he was alone, before moving out of the shadows and darting across the courtyard. He had almost reached the door when an enormous Torc Allta stepped out of a doorway. Another door opened and the hook-handed bard appeared. The assassin glimpsed the red-haired girl standing behind him.

Blade whipped out his knife and whirled around, his back to the physician's door.

'Did you think you could escape me?' the Torc Allta grunted. His snout wrinkled as he smelt the morning air. 'You cannot run from me. You carry my mark on you: the mark of the beast.'

'The goddess chose well,' Rua said quietly. 'You could have climbed up when the eel passed, but you waited. That shows great courage.'

'I don't know what you're talking about,' Ken muttered, arms wrapped tightly around his body to prevent himself from shaking. It wasn't bravery that had prevented him from moving: it was fear. He had been too terrified to move. Ken looked from Rua to the shadowy shapes of the priests. 'Tell me what's going on. I want to know how I got here.'

The hooded priests, only the vaguest outlines of their faces visible, stared at Ken, but said nothing.

'These are the Silent Ones,' Rua said, stepping closer to Ken. 'Their voices are used only in praise of the goddess.'

'Well, I'm not moving until I get some answers.' Ken folded his arms across his chest and looked around at the group.

Rua spread his arms. 'I have no answers.'

'Then who does?'

Rua looked away, and Ken got the impression that he was speaking, though he heard no words. 'The Keeper,' Rua said finally, turning back to him, 'the Keeper will answer all your questions. Now come.' He walked away, moving silently. The priests fell into line behind him, following with hooded heads dipped, hands tucked into sleeves, like shadows over the stone.

Ken stood and watched as the last priest disappeared below

the edge of the rock. Then, realising that he was standing alone on the flat stone, he scrambled after them. He was glad to be still wearing his De Danann clothing from his last adventure — how long ago had that been? He tried to make sense of the past few hours ... although he knew it couldn't have been hours. The truth was that he simply didn't know how much time had passed.

Along with Paedur, Ragallach, Megan, Faolan and Colum the Earthlord, he and Ally had defeated Balor. In the final battle, the Emperor's palace had been destroyed and his evil reign broken forever. The following day Faolan had used his wind-magic to send them along the timewinds to their own land and time — to Ireland in the last few years of the twentieth century. He had been standing in his bedroom for less than a minute when he had been snatched away, pulled back to this desert place.

But while only a minute of his time had gone by, how much time had passed on the De Danann Isle? How would he know? The stars! Ken looked up into the heavens, trying to make sense of the stars. He thought he could make out the Pole Star, but the configurations were changed and twisted, and there was an unusually high number of shooting stars darting across the sky.

The red-haired boy hurried past the line of monks and fell into step beside Rua. 'Where are we going?'

'To the Keeper. And we must hurry,' the priest added, looking to the east. Ken followed the direction of his gaze and realised that the deep purple of the sky was lightening to a paler blue. 'Dawn is close,' the priest said, the fear in his voice audible.

'Do you fear the heat?'

The priest shook his head. 'Not the heat — though that can suck the moisture from a man and kill him in less than a day. No, when the sun rises, then the great beasts will appear from their nests and caves ... and hunt.'

Ken's mouth went dry. 'What sort of beasts?'

'Monsters,' Rua whispered, looking around quickly, his eyes wide and frightened, as if the very mention of their name could bring them. 'The earliest legends tell of their creation by the old gods, who abandoned them here when they grew too fearsome.'

'Monsters?' Ken murmured.

'Some legends claim that they are demons or gods defeated in battle and forced to wear the terrible beast form.' Rua smiled quickly, and spoke loudly, almost as if he was trying to convince himself. 'But that is nonsense of course. They are beasts and there are only a few left now, but in the past, these creatures ruled the earth. Their time is past, and they will soon be gone. Each day more and more of the creatures die in this accursed desert. When the sun is high, you can see their bones littering the plain — that is why this place is known as the Desert of Bones.' Reaching up to his neck he lifted out a long curved sliver of white dangling on a black cord. He dropped the loop of cord over Ken's head. 'It is said that if you wear a bone amulet of one of the creatures, then that creature's kin cannot attack you. You saved my life back there; perhaps this will save yours.' Ken lifted the bone in the palm of his hand, squinting to look at it in the poor light. At first he thought it was a finger-bone, but then he realised it was too long. He measured it against his hand: it stretched from just above his wrist to the tip of his middle finger, curving from a thick root to a sharp point. He realised with a start what it was.

'It is a tooth from the greatest of the beasts,' Rua said, confirming his suspicions.

Ken swallowed hard. He was looking at a dinosaur tooth. 'You... you took this from a living creature?'

Rua laughed softly. 'If it had been living I would not have been able to take it. The beast had been dead a day, maybe two, before we came upon the remains of the body.'

'This is a dinosaur tooth,' Ken breathed.

'I do not know the word, dinosaur.'

'It means "terrible lizard",' Ken explained.

'It is a good name. We call them the Laghairt.'

'The Laghairt.' Ken looked across the desolate desert, long shadows now racing before the rising sun. 'How many are left? What types?' he asked quickly.

'Less than ten different families: perhaps two hundred beasts in all. The grass eaters went first. Then the meat-eaters lived off their carcasses for a time. When that meat was gone the Laghairt fought, and the weakest were slain. Now only the strongest remain. They are savage killers. And they like to hunt men,' Rua added. 'They have discovered a taste for human meat.'

Dinosaurs. Living dinosaurs! The thought was terrifying. The last of the dinosaurs had died out more than sixty-four million years before the first humans had walked this earth.

'Have we far to go?' Ken struggled to keep his voice steady.

The bald priest nodded across a broad plain of undulating dunes to a clump of rock that rose like an island from a dusty sea of sand. 'Our community is there.'

'It doesn't look too far,' Ken said softly.

'Further than you think.' Rua pointed out a route through stones and pillars of rock. 'We're relatively safe until we reach that point. But once we're out in the open, we're exposed, and if one of the beasts is nearby ...' He didn't finish the sentence.

Ken tried to swallow, but this mouth and throat were dry, and sand scraped under his teeth. He couldn't think about what would happen if they were caught in the open by a hungry dinosaur.

~

The creature's simple brain knew few things: light and dark, hunger and pain. These were the emotions it was hatched with. Experience taught it some of the essentials for survival. It knew which creatures were good to eat and those to avoid. It knew the scent of poisoned water, the acrid odour of others of its ilk, the warm meaty perfume of flesh.

Everything it did was dictated by its simple emotions. When it was dark, it rested; when it was light it hunted and foraged for food. When it was hungry, it ate ... and on the few occasions it attempted to eat something which hurt it, it fought or fled.

It had no concept of time, though its knowledge of its surroundings was surprisingly detailed. It knew the locations of fresh water, it knew where to find shelter during the hottest part of the day but, most importantly, it knew where it could dine off fresh meat. It had feasted in that spot more than once, plucking the small wriggling, succulent morsels from the desert floor.

And it hungered now.

Spreading translucent wings that were forty metres from tip to tip, the creature soared, enormous jaws gaping, hundreds of razor white teeth glinting as it turned its narrow head to the south.

~

Rua spotted the creature first. The priest stopped so suddenly that Ken ran into him.

'What's wrong?' he mumbled, his mouth dry, tongue gritty with sand. He'd been walking across the desert for what seemed like hours, although he knew it was only a fraction of that time, but already his nose and forehead were stinging with sunburn and he knew he'd be red and blotchy soon.

Rua pointed into the north. Ken shaded his eyes and peered into the heavens. Against a sky the colour of warm metal, he spotted a tiny black spot.

'What is it?' he wondered, aloud, 'a bird?'

'Not a bird.' Rua caught Ken by the arm, and pulled him forward. 'Hurry, we must hurry.'

The urgency in the priest's voice stilled the boy's questions. He glanced over his shoulder and discovered that all but two of the priests were following closely behind. The others had struck out across the desert — running towards the creature. 'Two are running away,' he panted.

'Not running,' Rua snapped. 'They're trying to lead the Flying Devil away from us.'

Ken looked into the sky again. The creature was closer now, and he was able to make out some details. It was a bird ... and then he realised that it was too big to be a bird. 'It's a species of nathair,' he breathed, remembering the Fomor's flying serpents.

'Not a nathair,' Rua said. 'Though it is possible that the flying serpents are a distant relation to this creature. Look at it again: its wings are broader, finer, its head is narrower.'

Ken took a quick look, stumbled and would have fallen if Rua had not caught him. The priest was right, the creature was not a nathair. This was something else, something older, far older, far more terrifying. It was difficult to make out details, but he guessed that the Laghairt was taller than a tall man, and its wingspan was enormous. There was no tail. 'It's a pterosaur,' he whispered, 'a flying reptile.' He knew that many pterosaurs were small, some of them no bigger than a sparrow, while one of the largest, the pteranodon, had a wingspan of five metres. But this creature was bigger — much, much bigger — than that. He knew then that it had to be the creature known as Quaetzalcoatlus, which had lived in the area that would one day be known as the United States and Mexico. Ken remembered the name, because Quaetzacoatal was another name for the Incan god, Kukalkan the Feathered Serpent, and Ken had always thought that Kukalkan sounded remarkably like Cuchulain, the great Irish hero.

The reptile's dark shadow slid over the dunes, rippling across the sands, mouth open to reveal a length of glistening tongue and hundreds of white teeth.

'Run,' Rua gasped, 'run for your life.' He pointed towards a dark opening in the rocks directly ahead.

Ducking his head down, keeping his elbows in tight, Ken fixed on the clump of rocks and pounded towards it, realising that the dark shadows in the stone were windows and doors. Sweat popped out in his hair-line, only to dry instantly, and he could actually feel his tongue swelling in his head. He had taken less than forty steps before he realised that he wasn't going to make it. His breath was fire in his lungs, his stomach heaving and churning, his legs felt like jelly. He was still twenty paces from the opening in the rocks when he fell. He hadn't even got the breath to cry out. Above the pounding of his head, he could hear the slow, steady slapping clap of the pterosaur's enormous wings and smell its stale, musty odour.

~

The creature had fed in this place before, snatching the wriggling, tasty meat. Instinct and experience had taught it that the creatures appeared in the time between dark and full light. They always congregated around the clump of stone in the centre of the desert. It had flown over this place in the past and the wriggling creatures had been absent, but its memory was short and it remembered only that it had tasted flesh here.

As it swooped out of the heavens, its keen sight spotted the line of wriggling creatures. Tilting its wings slightly, instinctively adjusting the flow of air against the delicate membranes, it fell towards the earth, its enormous black eyes fixed on the easy target of one who lay still and unmoving. Experience had also taught it that soft meat was the tastiest.

~

Ken rolled over onto his back. Two of the silent monks stood in the pterosaur's path, waving at the reptile, trying to attract its attention, but it ignored them. It was so low now that its wingtips touched the sand with every beat, leaving currents and eddies of sand in the air as it flew. It swept through the monks, its wings brushing them aside as if they were weightless. Rua attempted to distract it, but was struck to the ground by a flailing wing.

It was coming ... this way!

Ken realised with a terrified start that the creature was coming for him, claws poised, jaws gaping. Without the breath to scream he frantically rolled to one side... and the pterosaur's claws bit into the dune where he had lain seconds before. The tip of a wing caught him across the back as he tumbled away, the force of the blow numbing his shoulder, driving him face first into the sand.

The reptile's wings flapped, flapped and flapped again, as it attempted to build up speed. When it realised that it was unable to take off, it folded its wings and settled on the dunes in an explosion of sand. Then, with head ducked between hunched wings, like an enormous vulture, it turned to look at Ken. Opening its beak it emitted a raucous hiss and hopped closer. It jabbed at him, striking the sands when he jerked his foot back, its beak digging into the soft ground. It jabbed again, and he barely managed to roll aside. Its beak gouged an ugly rent where he had been lying. The flying lizard shifted its wings and, with a massive hop, landed right beside Ken. It hissed once before it drew its head back ... and the pterosaur erupted into flame.

Paedur stepped out of the doorway. 'There is no escape,' he said
softly. 'All the exits are blocked. Put down your weapons. You
are surrounded.'

Warriors, wearing chain-mail and the colours of the bardic
college appeared from the side streets, spears, swords and crossbows readied, levelled at the assassin.

Blade pulled out another knife, holding it awkwardly with his
injured right hand. 'Keep back,' he snapped. He flipped the knife
in his good hand, holding it by the blade so that he could throw
it.

'You have been bitten by a were-beast,' Paedur said, taking a
step closer. Blade lifted his knife and the young bard stopped.
'Unless you are treated, then by nightfall the were-curse will
have worked its way through your body and you will be beyond
help. The next time the moon rises full in the night sky, you will
take on the form of a Torc Allta. Many do not survive their first
were-change. And what happens if you do survive: you will
become an outcast, hunted by both men and beasts.'

'Give yourself up,' Ally said gently. 'We can treat your
wounds,' though even as she was speaking she turned to look at
Ragallach. She didn't know if the wound could be treated.

Ragallach nodded his huge head. 'You don't have much time
left,' he grunted. 'Unless you receive the proper treatment by the
time the sun touches noon, then you will be doomed.' His teeth

bared in a snarling grin. 'Even for the Torc Allta, every were-change is agony. You would not survive the pain of shifting bones and tearing muscles.'

'And what is the price of treatment?' Blade demanded.

'Information,' Paedur said coldly. 'The name of the person who hired you.'

'I don't have that information,' Blade said, sweat running from beneath his thinning hair, trickling across his cheeks and gathering on the point of his chin. 'Assassins never know the names of their employers. It's safer that way.'

'I know that,' Paedur smiled. 'But you can tell us how they made contact with you, or who contacted you, and then we will ask that person how contact was made with them ... and so, eventually we will trace the thread back to the beginning.'

'I will tell you nothing!' Blade snapped.

'Then you are doomed,' Paedur said simply. He raised his hook and the soldiers gathered closer.

There was a rasp of metal as locks and bolts suddenly slid home behind the assassin and the heavy door swung inwards. Blade swung around, thinking he was about to be attacked from behind. But the figure that stepped out of the shadows shocked everyone into silence.

It was a woman. The overall impression she gave was one of greyness. Her leather leggings and mail jerkin were grey, the matched swords she held in either gloved hand were grey, even her high riding boots were of soft grey leather. Cold grey eyes looked around the group before fixing on the the companions who were staring at her in horror. The woman's thin lips parted in a smile, revealing white teeth that had been filed to points.

'I see you remember me,' she hissed, looking from Paedur to Ally and Ragallach.

'Scathach,' Paedur said quietly, 'the Grey Warrior.' He took a slow step backwards, his every instinct warning him that something was very wrong. He had twenty armed guards with him — but even they would be no match for the fearsome warrior. 'You fought for Balor,' he said, simply to give himself time to think. He saw Ragallach put his paw on Ally's shoulder and gently pull her backwards.

'But now Balor is no more,' Scathach said, her razor sharp teeth turning her face into a hideous mask. 'And this land has no ruler.'

'The Lords of the Elements will rule,' the bard said quickly, 'as their ancestors did in the past.'

'Faolan the Windlord and Colum the Earthlord,' Scathach said, 'are little more than children. They are unfit to rule ... but so was Balor,' she added. She paused and added very softly. 'So I have decided to rule in their place!'

'You must be mad!' Ally said quickly.

The warrior woman smiled again. 'Why do you think I supported Balor? It was not out of any loyalty to him, and not because of the coin he paid me. No, it was simply to get close to him, to take control of his armies and eventually his city. If you had not destroyed the Emperor, then — sooner or later — I would have.'

'You *are* mad,' Paedur murmured. 'I suppose you sent this assassin to kill us?'

Scathach turned her head slightly to look at Blade who was leaning back against the wall, sweat streaming down his face. He had sheathed both knives and was now holding his right hand with his left. The skin had turned almost completely black, coarse reddish hairs sprouting from it. The Grey Warrior looked at Paedur again. 'Yes, I did. You and your companions are irritations, dangerous irritations. Balor made the mistake of underestimating you. I will not make that mistake.'

Paedur gestured at Blade with his hook. 'It seems you already did. He did not succeed.'

'I did not think he would,' Scathach said surprisingly. 'His real mission was to lead you here!' And then Scathach laughed, the sound echoing off the stones. 'You fools — you have walked into a trap!' Lifting her matched swords above her head, she clashed them together and screamed, 'Attack, attack!'

Paedur turned to shout a warning — but suddenly all the doors and windows were opening and dozens of creatures shambled out into the courtyard. Perhaps they had once been human, but some dark magic had changed and altered them, turning their skins the colour of old stone, leaving their eyes milky-white without colour, lengthening and sharpening their incisors into fangs, stretching their nails into talons.

'Vampir!' Paedur shouted. 'Don't let them bite you.'

One of the creatures caught a guard and spun him around. The man lifted his hand to defend himself — and immediately the vampir bit into the soft flesh of his wrist. The soldier screeched in pain and fear ... and then stopped suddenly, jerking upright, colour leaving his flesh, turning it first white, then grey, the pupils of his eyes paling to whiteness, his lips drawing back over long fang-like teeth that sprouted in either corner of his mouth. He lifted his hands, and nails flowed from the fingertips. Dropping his spear, he reached for the soldier standing beside him and bit into his shoulder, and immediately he too started to change.

One of the dead-eyed creatures appeared behind Ally, arms outstretched, hands curled into deadly claws. The stench of something old and mouldy and long-dead alerted the girl and she turned, but before she could draw breath to scream, Ragallach had caught the vampir by the ragged remains of its clothing, picked it up and flung it into the rest of the creatures. They fell to the ground in a tumble of arms and legs. They thrashed around before they rose to their feet and advanced again. And Ally realised then that they had made no sound.

Scathach laughed again. 'You see bard, you cannot stand against me. I command an army of vampir. This is an army that cannot be slain, an army that finds new recruits day by day. Soon, Baddalaur will be a city of vampir ... and then I will advance on Falias. By the time the seasons turn, the entire De Danann Isle will be mine!'

'Retreat, retreat,' Paedur called. He waited in the mouth of the alleyway until the last of the few surviving soldiers had slipped past him. He was shocked to discover that more than half the men had been lost and were now vampir.

'Run bard, run. You cannot defeat me. I will rule this isle, and then I will conquer the known world!'

'Balor had similar plans,' Paedur reminded the Grey Warrior.

'Balor was a fool,' she snapped. 'He did not have the gods on his side. My gods have given me the gift of these undead vampir.' She stretched out her left hand, her curved sword pointed directly at the bard. 'You will join my vampir army, I swear it.'

Without a word, Paedur turned and joined Ally and Ragallach in the alleyway, leaving Scathach and Blade and the vampir alone in the courtyard. The Grey Warrior crouched beside the assassin who had slumped to the ground. The small man's dark eyes widened in fear.

'You have a choice,' Scathach snapped, 'join me as my general — or I will allow the were-curse to take you.'

'That's not much of a choice,' Blade said weakly.

The woman glanced over her shoulder at the milling vampir. 'I could always make you one of them,' she said almost gently.

'I think I'll join you,' Blade said immediately.

The flaming pterosaur crashed into the sand and disintegrated, cinders and ash settling over Ken in a choking cloud. Scrambling to his feet, he staggered away from the lizard which was now nothing more than a pile of white ash and blackened charred bones. He rubbed the back of his hand across his mouth — his lips and tongue were coated in the foul-tasting ash — and turned, just as Rua caught his arm and pulled him away from the carcass.

'The smoke and smell of burning meat will attract others,' the bald priest panted. 'We must hurry.'

'But what happened?' Ken demanded. 'What happened?'

Rua shook his head. He pointed high into the sky and Ken saw a dozen black dots circling in the air. He was about to say 'birds,' when he realised that he hadn't seen any birds in the desert. 'More Flying Devils?' he asked.

'The rest of the nest,' Rua agreed.

The outcropping of stone was nearer now, and Ken could make out some details. It was a building, though whether it was natural or man-made was impossible to say. There were no sharp edges, no corners to the shape and the stones looked as if they had melted together to form a smooth hump. Tiny slit windows were cut into the stone, and the doorway seemed unnaturally narrow and was set up off the ground.

A high-pitched cawing scream drifted down, and a triangular shape flew across the sun, its shadow rippling over the sands.

Ken risked a quick glance upwards and felt his stomach heave: the pterosaurs were nearer now. He counted eight ... and they were all bigger than the single creature which had attacked them.

'Not much further,' Rua whispered, pulling him along.

The first of the priests reached the door. He turned sideways and slid through the narrow opening. Ken looked at the building again and realised that the windows were closing, stone shutters fitting neatly into the openings, sealing them. Another priest slid through the door and then another.

A pterosaur flew low overhead, the beat of its wings ruffling the sand, a musty stale odour filling the air.

'Why don't they attack?' Ken gasped.

'They will,' Rua promised, as they ran into the shadow cast by the building. 'But the smoke and fire have confused them. When they realise one of their own has been slain they will go wild. Now, turn and slide through the door,' he added, with obvious relief.

Ken twisted his body sideways, and took a crab-like step through the narrow opening. It was so cold and dark inside the mound that he was momentarily blind and immediately started to shiver. Someone threw a blanket over his shoulders and pressed a sponge to his face. Ice cold water ran down his chin and curled along his throat, soothing his dry skin. It felt delicious. When he opened his eyes again, he could make out the shapes of the monks surrounding him. Rua remained silhouetted against the door, staring out anxiously. 'Come on Robh,' he called, his voice echoing in the stone chamber.

Ken ducked down and peered out through the opening. One priest remained outside. Ken recognised him as one of the men who had tried to lead the pterosaurs away. He had turned back and was running towards the mound, head ducked, arms pumping by his side, feet digging deeply into the sand.

But the Flying Devils were close behind.

A pterosaur swept past, low enough for the wind from its wings to buffet the man to the ground. He rolled smoothly to his feet and kept running.

'Run Robh, run!' Rua called.

'Help him,' Ken said urgently, tugging at the priest's sleeve. 'You have to help him.'

'We cannot.'

'You must!' Ken insisted.

'We have no weapons here,' Rua said softly, not looking at him. He drew his breath sharply as one of the lizards flew close enough to knock the priest down again. It jabbed at him with its beak and both Rua and Ken saw the bright flash of blood as he fell.

'Something burned the pterosaur that was after me,' Ken said shrilly. 'Use that!'

Robh was running again, but weaving from side to side, one hand pressed against his side.

'I cannot,' Rua whispered, eyes sparkling mistily. Then he suddenly squeezed his eyes shut and looked away. Ken looked through the door again. Robh the priest had vanished, but high in the sky, wings flapping furiously, the boy saw that one of the pterosaurs had something in its beak. It wriggled for a little while, then stopped.

'I'm sorry,' Ken said, realising how empty the phrase sounded.

Rua nodded. He wiped his eyes on the back of his sleeve and tried to smile. 'He did not cry out. He kept his oath to the Goddess to the very end. And he died in her service. We will add his name to the list of martyrs. I am proud of him.'

'Was he a friend?' Ken asked.

'He was my brother.'

~

'I am Foltor.'

Ken turned his head. A stick-thin old man stood in the doorway. Like Rua, he was completely bald and his smooth shining skull contrasted sharply with his heavily lined face. His skin was the colour of old leather, but his teeth were startling white, and against his tanned skin, his blue eyes blazed brilliantly.

'I am the Abbot here.'

Ken tried to sit up but his muscles protested and he lay back on the hard stone bed with a groan.

Foltor came forward and stretched out a tiny hand. Ken reached for it, and the old man drew him up with surprising ease.

'I'm Ken ... Kenneth Morand,' the young man said. 'I didn't mean to fall asleep,' he added.

'There is no shame in it,' Foltor said easily. 'You were exhausted after your long journey and it was only natural that you should sleep. Sleep allows the body to heal itself.'

'I ... I'm sorry about Robh,' Ken said softly.

'Why?' Foltor asked, surprising him.

Ken shook his head, suddenly unsure what to say.

'Robh served the Goddess well. He dedicated his life to her and died in her service. He is assured of his reward. Do not mourn his death, he did not die in vain. He got you here safely.'

'Me!'

Foltor nodded. 'It took us four days to find you, and then, when we had located your position on the Red Cliffs, we were forced to wait another two days for the sandstorms to die down before we could send out a rescue party.'

'You were looking for me? Why?'

Foltor smiled and shook his head. 'So many questions, so many questions. Let me ask you a question first: would you like to eat? To wash?'

'Yes,' Ken said simply.

'Then follow me.'

Foltor turned and ducked through the low entrance to the small bedchamber Rua had shown him to earlier. Ken squeezed through and hurried after the old man, his footsteps echoing off the smooth corridor. 'Why did you make all the doors so small?' he grumbled.

'We didn't,' Foltor said with a smile. 'This mound was ancient before the first man or beast set foot on the De Danann Isle. It was built by a people who used a magic that is as yet unknown to us. These corridors for example,' he said, waving an arm around, 'are perfectly circular, the floor meets wall and wall meets ceiling without any evidence of a crack or join. It is as if a hot pin was driven through a wax candle.' He pointed to a door as they walked past. 'The doors were built for a different frame to ours. As far as we can determine, the race who built this mound were smaller than human-kind and slender. We recently discovered some hieroglyphs which suggest that they may have been insectile in appearance.'

'What happened to them?' Ken wondered.

'No-one knows. They simply vanished.'

'And when did you move in?' Ken asked.

'The Priesthood of the Goddess have lived in this mound for nearly five hundred generations.'

'Five hundred generations,' Ken said slowly, trying to work out how many years that represented.

Foltor led Ken through another narrow door into a circular chamber. A round open skylight in the ceiling shed a golden circle of light onto a pool of still black water. 'You will find a robe in that alcove,' Foltor said. 'When you have finished, follow the corridor to its end. I will be waiting there. I will have food and drink in readiness.'

As the priest turned away, Ken caught his arm. 'The pterosaur...' he began, and stopped when Foltor frowned. 'The Flying Devil. What happened to it? When it burst into flames,' he added.

'The fire magic destroyed it,' Foltor said simply.

'Fire magic?'

'We are the Silent Ones, the priests of the Goddess. We are the Keepers of the Flame.'

Understanding hit Ken like a blow to the pit of the stomach. 'You are the Firelords!'

'No,' Foltor said with a smile, 'we are merely priests. You are the Firelord.'

Paedur sat down at the wooden table and looked from Ally to Ragallach. His thin face was paler than usual and Ally noticed that his dark eyes were troubled. 'How bad is it?' she asked.

'We're getting reports from all over the city,' he said quietly. He worked at a splinter in the table with his hook. 'Vampir are everywhere. There is panic in the streets. People are barricaded behind locked doors, and the bards have been forced to seal the college gates because they could take in no more refugees.'

'Vampir.' Ragallach shook his head. 'The Unliving.'

'You know what vampir are?' Paedur asked, turning to Ally.

'In my time they are a myth, creatures from a horror story or a movie ...' she stopped, realising that neither of her companions would understand what a movie was. She frowned, trying to remember what she knew about vampires, though she noticed that both Paedur and Ragallach pronounced it slightly differently to her, making it a shorter, harsher sound. 'They are the Undead. They drink blood. They're not supposed to be able to walk in sunlight, they fear garlic and the symbol of the cross ... I always thought they were a legend, I never believed they actually existed,' she added shakily.

Ragallach grunted. 'They exist.' He rubbed a paw against his bristled chin, the sound harsh and rasping. 'Even amongst the were-clans the vampir are feared. We call them dearg-due, the red blood-suckers. They haunt the camp fires at night and there are places — ruined villages, abandoned castles — that the dearg-due claim as theirs. None of the Clan Allta, the were-clans, will venture there.' He turned to look at Paedur with his tiny pink eyes and his heavy brow creased in a frown. 'Ally's right — how can the vampir walk during the daylight hours?'

'I wondered about that too,' Paedur murmured. 'I've been looking into the myths. It is not entirely true that the vampir can only move about at night. Although their powers are much weakened during the daylight hours, they can walk abroad during the day, provided they are not exposed to the glare of the noonday sun. Once they keep to the shadows, they will be relatively safe.'

'When the vampir attacked us this morning, the courtyard was in shadow from the surrounding buildings,' Ally said quickly.

Paedur nodded. 'I know. But I don't think that's the only reason these particular ones are out in daytime. I don't think these are true vampir,' he added. 'I'm not even sure they were dead.'

'They looked dead to me ...' Ally began, and then stopped. She had never seen a dead person before in her life!

'I believe these are ordinary people held under a vampir spell,' Paedur continued. 'They look and act like blood-suckers, and that is why they can turn ordinary people into creatures like themselves so quickly ...' His voice trailed away and his expression grew distant, dreamy. 'And Scathach is dominating them, controlling the spell ... I wonder?' he whispered.

'What?' Ally asked.

Paedur's eyes snapped open. 'I was wondering if Scathach was a Baobhan Sith.'

Ragallach drew in his breath in a quick horrified gasp.

'What's a Baobhan Sith?' Ally ventured, the fear in the Torc Allta's voice and sudden alarm in the bard's eyes frightening her.

'A Baobhan Sith is a Vampir Queen,' he said simply.

'Is that possible?' Ally asked.

'I've never thought about it before,' Paedur said, 'but when you weigh up the evidence it begins to make sense. Her skin is grey, like the vampir we saw earlier,' Paedur said.

'And all her teeth are filed to points,' Ragallach added, 'but that might be to hide sharp incisors, the true mark of the vampir.'

The bard nodded. 'And we know she's fast and deadly. Vampir are supposed to be inhumanly fast.' He nodded again. 'It all makes sense: the Grey Warrior is a Baobhan Sith. The ancient legends are full of the exploits of the creatures. They fought with the human-kind and were wiped out in a great battle more than five hundred years ago.'

'Well not all of them died,' Ragallach snapped. He stood up and strode across to the slit window and peered out over the large town that surrounded the College of Baddalaur. It was close to noon now, and the twisting narrow streets should have been alive with people. From this height he should have been hearing a low droning, like the humming of a distant hive, and smelt the countless odours wafting up from below. The Torc Allta's damp snout wrinkled. All it could smell from the deserted streets below was blood and fear.

'What is happening in the town?' Ally asked.

Paedur stood up and joined Ragallach. Without turning around he said, 'The townspeople are being turned into vampir. First one person is bitten and they in turn bite two and those two bite two more ... It won't be long before everyone is infected by the hideous curse. And once they are vampir, they are under the control of the Vampir Queen. She could control the entire population of Baddalaur in a matter of days.'

'And what then, I wonder?' Ragallach murmured.

'She will send her army out to take the capital, Falias. An army of vampir would be virtually indestructible. Nothing could stand in its way. She could turn the De Danann Isle into a vampir isle within a matter of seasons.' He shuddered. 'In ancient times, the vampir kept the human-kind for food and drink, in much the same way as we now keep cattle.'

'What can we do?' Ragallach asked.

'I'm not sure,' Paedur murmured.

'We have to stop her!' Ally snapped. 'We defeated Balor, we can stop Scathach.'

The young bard and the beast turned to look at her. Brushing strands of red hair from her eyes, she put her hands on her hips and stared at them. 'It's simple: Scathach is a vampire — sorry, *vampir* — Queen. If we defeat her, then the spell will be broken and everyone returns to normal.' She shrugged.

'First we have to stop Scathach,' Paedur reminded her.

'Ally's right,' Ragallach said, moving away from the window to stand behind the girl. He put his heavy paw on her shoulder. 'We can't let the Baobhan Sith get away with this. We have to stand against her. If we don't,' he added, 'then the human-kind will be wiped out ... and the non-humans will surely follow.'

Paedur looked as if he was about to argue, then he simply closed his mouth and nodded. 'You're right of course.'

Ally chewed on her bottom lip. 'We're agreed. We're going to need some help,' she said decisively.

Paedur nodded. 'We'll need Faolan, Colum and Megan. Their skills will help us now.'

Ally held up one finger. 'There is one other who might help us,' she said tentatively.

Paedur looked at Ragallach. 'Who?' they said together.

'Cichal the Fomor!'

'Cichal?' Paedur demanded.

'He helped us escape to the Fomor Isles, didn't he?' Ally said. Paedur nodded.

'Can the *vampir* drink Fomor blood, serpent's blood?'

Paedur looked at the Torc Allta, who shrugged his massive shoulders. 'I don't know,' the bard finally admitted. 'I've never heard of a vampir Fomor ...' His voice trailed away as he considered the implications. Ally was right of course; the Fomor were ideal. Virtually invincible, they were a terrifying fighting force who didn't know the meaning of fear. But would they fight alongside the human-kind, their sworn enemy?

'As soon as Faolan arrives here, we will fly for the Fomor Isles, and seek their assistance,' he said decisively.

'But what about Ken?' Ally said, 'when can we look for him? You said he was in the desert.'

Paedur stepped forward and looked into Ally's wide green eyes. 'There is nothing we can do for Ken at the moment,' he said gently. 'We have to stop Scathach before she wipes all human-kind from the De Danann Isle.'

In the cellar of a rotting house at the very edges of Baddalaur, the Grey Warrior sat cross-legged in darkness. All around her she could hear the restless movement of some of her newfound army. No-one spoke, because she had not given them permission to speak, and the only sounds were the constant plinking and tinkling of dripping water.

Although there was no light in the basement, Scathach closed her eyes to visualise the three wild gods she honoured: Hiisi, the Lord of Evil, Kalma, the Goddess of Death and Tuomi, the God of the Underworld. She had worshipped this unholy trinity of vampir gods from the first day she had taken up a sword. She had dedicated her life to them, and in turn they had made her powerful and deadly.

Scathach was the last of the Baobhan Sith, whom mortal men called vampir. She was determined that she would not remain alone for very much longer. By dawn, she would control the town. It wasn't a large town, but it held the famous bardic college, and represented the centre of all knowledge. Soon all the De Danann Isle would be talking about the return of the vampir to the isle. Eventually, the island would be hers, and a Baobhan Sith would rule the Isle of the Goddess again.

The vampir had ruled the De Danann Isles before the human-kind had walked the world, even before the Fomor had come up from their islands to fight for the lush land. Legends claimed that the vampir had come from an ice-locked land at the top of the world, or from the mysterious highlands of a distant continent, or even from a world beyond the stars, but no-one knew for certain and the true history of the Baobhan Sith race had died with the race. Scathach alone had survived, hiding amongst the human-kind for many hundreds of years, constantly moving on when the short-lived warm-bloods began to realise that she did not age. But Scathach had sworn a great oath that she would restore the vampir as rulers, first of the De Danann Isle, and then of the known world. She had been going to allow Balor to fight her battles for her, because she knew that she could easily control the Emperor. Those plans had changed when Balor had been defeated.

However, her new plan was better — much better. She would use the humans to fight against themselves.

'I will make the vampir great again,' she said aloud.

But first she had to defeat the bard and his companions.

'Blade,' she called, her voice harsh and demanding.

Light moved on the stairs and the small assassin appeared, a sputtering torch held high over his head. The shadows danced across his features, giving his face a skull-like appearance. 'You called for me, my lady.' He squinted into the darkest corner of the room, where he thought the Grey Warrior was crouching. When she spoke again however, her voice came from the opposite corner of the rotting cellar.

'Take a dozen vampir,' she commanded, 'and bring me the bard and his companions. I want them alive and unharmed,' she added. 'I want to have the pleasure of adding them to my collection of slaves.'

'Yes, my lady,' Blade said immediately.

'And remember,' Scathach said softly, 'it is only my power which keeps the were-curse from claiming your body.'

Blade touched the metal and stone collar he now wore against his throat. The Grey Warrior had locked it around his neck, claiming that it alone could keep the were spell at bay. She also told him that the power in the collar needed to be renewed regularly. If it wasn't, then the were-curse would turn him into a Torc Allta, a were-boar. Blade realised that he was as much a slave to the Grey Warrior as the humans whom she had turned into blood-suckers.

'Do not fail me,' Scathach called as Blade trudged up the stairs. 'And remember, I want them alive and unharmed.'

Ken padded down the smoothly polished corridor, his bare feet leaving wet impressions on the dark dusty stone. Water dripped from the damp ends of his tangled red hair. He was dressed in the simple cotton robe he had found waiting for him when he'd climbed out of the pool, and he carried his clothes and shoes tucked under his arm.

He found Foltor waiting for him in a small circular room at the end of the corridor. The room was bare except for a round stone table and two high backed stone chairs. The old man had his back to the door and was standing with his hands clasped behind his back. He was staring through the narrow slit window at the pterosaurs which still circled in the cloudless sky outside.

'There is a legend,' he said suddenly, without turning around, 'that the gods made the Laghairt and Flying Devils before they made men and beasts. Then, realising their mistakes, they destroyed the beasts and tried again. Now, there are some religions which believe that their gods are infallible, that they do not make mistakes, and so they do not hold with this belief. They consider that everything evil and bad in this world was made by demons ... or men.' He turned suddenly, bright blue eyes twinkling. 'What do you think?'

Caught off guard, Ken stared at the old man for a moment, then said, 'In my time we believe in evolution ... that is the gradual change of men and beasts from other creatures.'

'I have heard this theory,' Foltor said, surprising him, 'but it does not address the question: do you believe that the gods make mistakes?'

Ken stared at him blankly.

'You do believe in a god or gods?'

'Well ... yes, in a god.'

'And did this god of yours ever make a mistake?'

'I don't know,' the boy admitted.

Foltor turned away from the window and sat in one of the high-backed chairs. 'Sit, please.' He gestured to chunks of bread on carved wooden plates and a sweating pitcher of water. 'Eat, drink.'

'I want to know what's going on,' Ken said, breaking off a corner of the bread and biting into it. It tasted of dark sugar and a cinnamon spice.

'Of course you do. And it is only right that you should know. While you eat and drink your fill, allow me to tell you what I know. I don't know all the details ...' He raised a hand when Ken opened his mouth to speak. 'However, my story will answer a lot of your questions.'

The boy nodded. He poured water from the jug into a wooden mug and sipped slowly.

'I know a lot about you, Kenneth of the Clan Morand, and of your sister, Alison. I know you are both from the Time to Come, though exactly how far in the future I do not know. I have looked into this future and have seen the terrible times you live in, with poisoned air, foul water, hunger, thirst and disease claiming much of the world. It saddens me to think that this is what this world will become.'

'You should know that we think this is a terrible place ...' Ken muttered.

Foltor locked his fingers together and stared into the boy's eyes. 'The air is clean. The water drinkable. No nation thirsts or starves and our physicians can cure diseases that baffle your doctors and healers.' He spread his hands. 'There are evil people in this time, creatures like Balor and some of the Fomor, though not as many as you might think. Are there no evil people in your time?'

Ken nodded slowly.

'There are no good times ... only good people. In your time, as in this, there are good people, people who care about their world, and the future.'

Ken frowned, wondering where all this was leading.

'The ancient gods of the De Danann Isle cared too. They were human-kind before they became gods, and they lived in a time which was infinitely more dangerous than this, a time of terrible beasts and terrifying wild magic.'

Foltor leaned back in the chair, tilted his head back and closed his eyes.

'In time they conquered this land and tamed the beasts. They laid the foundations of what would eventually become the four cities of the De Danann Isle: Falias, Gorias, Finias and Murias. They established the arts of the culture of this great island.'

'Where did they come from?' Ken wondered aloud.

'Who knows?' Foltor said. 'That is the mystery. Around them were nothing but savages, more ape than man, cousins to the Simpean-sai and Chopts. But these people were beautiful; tall, elegant, with the slanting, uptilted eyes and the sharp features you can still find in the oldest De Danann families.

'There were twelve or possibly thirteen families then. Each of these ruling clans took on the task of mastering one craft or skill: some practised medicine, metalwork, stonecraft, gemwork, farming, while others specialised in the magical skills.' The old man smiled thinly. 'It was a clever way of ensuring that each family became expert in that particular field ... and it also ensured that all the original settlers worked together, because all their skills were needed to make the settlement a success.

'Many of these original De Danann folk are now worshipped as gods by the present day inhabitants. That is how most gods begin, but to survive, gods need men to worship them, and the more people who believe in them, the stronger the gods become. There is a very ancient saying, "faith lends substance". It means that the more you believe in something, the more likely it will be to happen. If you believe in a god or demon, then the god or demon will come into existence. The De Danann gods survive because people believe in them.'

Ken smiled, and Foltor sat forward suddenly.

'You doubt me?' he asked softly.

Taken by surprise, the boy could only shake his head. 'I don't know. I've seen magic on this island, so I suppose it must be true.'

Foltor picked up a piece of bread. 'What do you see?'

'Bread,' Ken said.

'Nothing more?'

'No.'

'I see a chunk of stone, pitted and scarred, tiny reflective crystals embedded in its surface,' Foltor said slowly. 'Look at it again, and see the stone ...'

Ken looked at the bread ... and watched as it slowly hardened into a piece of aged granite. Flat slivers of silica sparkled as Foltor turned it.

'You see the stone because I have told you it is there, and in your own small way, you believe it to be true. Perhaps you think I've magicked it; I assure you, I have not. It is only your belief which has made this piece of bread into stone.' Foltor broke off a corner of the stone and popped it into his mouth. At that precise moment, Ken remembered he was looking at bread, and the torn loaf returned.

'What does this prove?' Ken asked.

'That men make gods out of men,' Foltor said softly, 'and that no man is infallible. Men make mistakes. The De Danann gods knew there was only one real threat to the existence of the De Danann Isle, and that was the Elemental Magics, those uncontrollable forces of earth and air, fire and water. So the gods entrusted the four greatest De Danann families with the secret of controlling the magic. 'And that is where they made their mistake.'

'What mistake?' Ken asked.

'They should have destroyed the Elemental lore instead of passing it on. By placing it in the hands of individual families — the Elemental Lords — they made those families vulnerable to attack by people like Balor who wanted to use the lore for themselves.'

'But Balor is dead,' Ken interrupted.

'And he has been replaced by an even more deadly foe: Scathach the Grey Warrior.'

Ken nodded. 'I know her ...'

'No, you do not!' Foltor snapped. 'She is more — much more — than a simple warrior. She is Baobhan Sith — a vampir! She was using Balor as a way of gaining control of the isle. Now that he is gone, she has already started to raise an army to march on Falias. An army of vampir.' He stopped and drew in a deep breath. 'But that is another tale. Where was I ... oh yes, the Elemental Lords. The Lords separated to the four corners of the island where they were treated like kings. Usually, they used their magic for good, though more often they did not use their magic at all. And these four powerful families never met because of an ancient prophecy which said that the Elemental Lords would only meet again at the end of the world when they would gather to save the world. They believed that by not meeting, the world would never end.'

Ken chewed the bread and watched the old man closely, realising that there was something he wasn't saying.

'Well, we are the Priests of the Goddess. We believe that these are the last days of the De Danann Isle.

'When Faolan the Windlord and Colum the Earthlord were brought together, we knew the prophecy was coming true.' Foltor smiled icily. 'You thought you were carried to this time by an accident of wild magic.' The priest shook his bald head. 'You were brought here deliberately, Kenneth of the Clan Morand, because the blood of the Firelords runs in your veins. When you traced out the ancient prayer spiral on the pillar on the Avenue of Stones you awoke the Goddess Danu. She recognised you for what you were, and then communicated this information to me in dreams.'

Ken was shaking his head but Foltor ignored him.

'When Balor misused Colum's power, he damaged the very binding that holds this isle together. Deep underground, molten stone and white hot mud are bubbling to the surface. It will take a Firelord — a master Firelord — to quench the flames. You must become that Firelord.'

'I cannot.'

'Faith,' Foltor said quickly. 'Faith lends substance. You must master the firelore. The survival of the entire island depends upon it.'

Ally sat on the hard wooden bench and looked at the beautifully drawn map of the De Danann Isles. Her fingers moved over the rough surface of the painted leather hide, circling the area Paedur had called the Desert of Bones.

Ken was somewhere here.

Closing her eyes, she breathed deeply, trying to see her brother's face clearly in her mind. 'Ken,' she whispered, her voice the only sound in the empty library. 'Ken ... where are you Ken?' The last time she'd called for her brother, there had been the impression of heat and sand, but now there was nothing. A lump formed in the back of her throat.

Where was he?

Was he still alive?

What had started out as a grand adventure had turned into a nightmare. Her brother was lost and they were both trapped: he in some scorching desert, she in a town that had been invaded by vampirs. She wished now that they had never walked down Skellig Michael's stone stairway and stepped into the past.

Ally opened her eyes and looked at the map again, tracing the route from Baddalaur to the Desert of Bones. It lay to the south and west of the college town, not far from Gorias, the coastal city. She knew very little about that part of the country except that Balor had used the Earthlord's magic to destroy much of Gorias. She had no idea of the scale of the map, so she couldn't work out how far away it was.

What was she going to do?

What could she do?

Find Ken.

Ally straightened, shocked by the simple thought. Find Ken. She couldn't ... it was too far ... she had no idea where ... she simply couldn't.

The girl took a deep breath, calming herself. What was stopping her from going to look for her brother? There was no-one here to tell her what to do. In this land and time, she made her own decisions. She suddenly found that freedom almost frightening.

Find Ken.

It would mean travelling across a wild and savage land with only this rough map to guide her. And she would be alone. Her friends had problems of their own, and she couldn't expect them to accompany her. And what would she do when she reached the Desert of Bones, how was she to locate her brother? Hadn't Paedur said that there was a link between her and her brother. Maybe the bard could give her something that would allow her to trace Ken. And if she found her brother, what then? How would they get back to Baddalaur ... how would they manage to return to their own time. But if they did, then Ally swore, they were never returning to the De Danann Isle again.

Ally was rolling up the map when she heard the distinctive chink of metal. She stood up, turning her head, pulling her thick red hair off her ear to listen. She was alone in the library; in fact, she was sure she was alone on this floor. The few townspeople who had escaped the vampir were gathered in the rooms below safe behind locked doors and windows. There were guards on the gates and walls. The Master Bards and Scholars were meeting in the Great Hall on the ground floor, trying to decide what they were going to do. Paedur and Ragallach were there with them.

Metal scraped again.

Moving as quietly as possible, Ally moved closer to the sound, stepping across the volumes piled high on the floor, moving between the tall bookshelves.

She could definitely hear something now. A metallic rasping, a gentle tapping — and then the distinctive crack as glass snapped. She froze, heart hammering. There was silence then for a long time, but just when she thought that the sounds had vanished, she heard metal squeak again — and this time she recognised the noise: it was the sound of metal scraping off glass. Peering through the tightly packed bookshelves, she carefully moved a book out of the way, allowing her to look across the room.

One of the long narrow slit windows was broken, tiny shards of coloured glass scattered on the floor.

Ally frowned. The room was on the fourth floor, so it was unlikely that someone had thrown a stone, but maybe something had flown into the glass — a bird, a lizard, a peist? But that still didn't account for the metallic sounds she had heard. There were no trees outside the window, so it couldn't have been a branch tapping off the glass. She was still peering through the bookshelves when the gloved hand appeared. Black clad fingers worked at the shards of glass around the simple lock, pulling them away, making the hole larger. Then a hand appeared, felt around for the lock and twisted it up. The window swung open.

And Blade climbed into the room.

Ally felt her breath catch in her throat, and her heart was now thumping so hard it threatened to make her sick.

The small dark man crouched on the floor, a long black-bladed knife in his hand. He kept turning his head from side to side, eyes bright, nostrils flaring. When he was satisfied that the room was empty, he straightened and looked out of the window. Ally saw then that a small metal hook was caught onto the windowsill. Blade had used the grappling hook to climb up the outside of the wall. She was just beginning to wonder if he was alone when a second figure appeared. Her stomach churned. The figure was a blank-eyed, fanged vampir. It was followed by a second and then a third.

Pressing both hands across her mouth to prevent herself from crying out, Ally backed away from the shelves. She had to warn the others. She was turning when her foot nudged a pile of books.

They tumbled to the floor in a cloud of choking dust. Her eyes watered and she sneezed. She turned and ran, scattering books and charts behind her.

'Who's there?' Blade's voice was calm and even, sounding as if he had every right to be in the room. 'Show yourself.'

Reaching the map table, she quickly gathered up the chart of the De Danann Isle and backed towards the door, eyes darting wildly.

Blade stepped around a bookshelf. He stared at the girl for a moment, then his thin lips curled in a smile as he raised his knife.

Ally darted through the narrow aisles between the shelves. A thin knife hissed into the books at her left, another bit into the wooden shelf to her right. She threw herself to the floor and crawled beneath a shelf, then rolled under another before coming to her feet and racing down an aisle.

The door.

Where was a door? She had become confused and lost her direction. Then, with a cold chill, she suddenly realised she had been running back towards the broken window.

She heard Blade's whispered instructions and the vampir's rasping breathing and realised that the others were trying to remain silent. They didn't want to make any noise. The girl grinned; obviously they didn't want anyone to know they were in Baddalaur. Tucking the map into her belt, she straightened. Planting her feet firmly, she placed both hands against a book-shelf and pushed. The shelf shifted, rocked and settled. Ally pushed again. Slowly, ponderously the shelf tilted over, ancient books, leather, metal and stone bound volumes crashing to the floor in a thunderous explosion. But even these sounds were swallowed as the shelf came crashing down onto another shelf, knocking it down onto a third shelf.

The noise was incredible, amplified by the small room. The remainder of the slit windows in the room shattered with the noise. Ally grinned; the entire college had probably heard the noise. She spotted the door and she scrambled across the book-strewn floor towards it.

A knife thudded into it just as she reached for the handle, and she jerked her hand away.

'Don't think you can escape so easily,' Blade whispered, reaching for another knife.

Ally ignored him and darted through the door, pulling it shut behind her. She had taken a dozen steps when the door scraped open and the corridor filled with the vampir's rasping breathing. Another knife clattered off the stones at her feet, showering sparks over her boots. She raced down the corridor, expecting to feel a vampir's hands on her throat, or the sting of its fangs.

'Stop,' Blade commanded, 'don't make me hurt you.'

Ally drew in a deep breath and then screamed, 'Vampir! Vampir. Paedur. Ragallach!'

She had almost reached the stairs when the first vampir caught her. She was briefly aware of the smell of the creature, and then a heavy hand fell onto her shoulder, the force of the blow driving her to her knees. She cowered, eyes squeezed tightly shut, expecting the creature's hands on her, its teeth sinking into her flesh. When nothing happened she opened her eyes and looked up. The female vampir was standing over her, long-nailed hands curled into claws. But the creature was looking around slowly, blank eyes wide and staring. Then, slowly, slowly, the vampir's eyes closed and she toppled to the ground to lie beside Ally. It was then the girl saw the sliver of wood protruding from the creature's neck. 'Megan!' she cried.

The young warrior maid appeared at the top of the stairs, blowpipe pressed to her lips. Ally saw her cheeks puff, and then she heard the hiss of the dart. Another vampir tumbled to the ground. Megan fired another two darts, bringing two more vampir to the ground, while Ally scrambled the rest of the way to the top step. She could hear noises from below, the tramp of booted feet, the clatter of weapons.

Megan fired another dart as a vampir reared up before her. The man crumpled sideways. Suddenly Blade appeared in front of the girl, a long knife in his hand. Before she had a chance to put another dart into the hollow tube, he lunged at her. She side-stepped and batted the knife away with the blowpipe, then brought it down on his head, snapping it in two. Dazed and shocked, Blade staggered backwards. He then turned and raced towards the library, calling the remainder of his vampir back with him. He stopped at the door and turned to glare at Ally and Megan. 'That's twice you've cheated me. But you will not escape a third time.' He slammed the door shut and the two girls heard wood scrape as shelves were piled against it.

The College Guards appeared on the stairs and poured into the corridor. They hammered on the thick door with their axes, quickly breaking it down, but by that time, Blade and his seven remaining vampir had escaped.

Megan sat on the top stair beside Ally and put her arm around her shoulder. The warrior maid's eyes were bright with excitement.

'When did you get back?' Ally asked shakily.

'Just in time,' Megan grinned.

'So we meet again,' Faolan said, rising to his feet as Megan and Ally came into the room. He pushed strands of golden hair out of his eyes and smiled broadly. 'It's good to see you again, Ally.'

'And you too Faolan,' she said softly. Looking at the boy — she thought he was about a year younger than herself — it was hard to realise that he was the Windlord, master of one of the elemental magics, capable of shaping and controlling the forces of air. She turned to the small, dark-skinned, dark-eyed boy sitting quietly before the blazing fire, warming himself. He smiled shyly, but didn't speak.

Ally returned his smile. 'Hello Colum.'

Colum was the Earthlord, master of the forces of earth. Although he was the same age as Faolan, he was only half his size. But she knew this tiny boy was capable of controlling enough force to rip the De Danann isle apart. Balor had taken the boy's mother and younger brother and sister prisoner in order to force Colum to use his magic. When the emperor had finally been defeated, Colum had used his magic to open the earth beneath the emperor's palace and swallow it.

Ragallach came up behind her and eased her into a high-backed chair. He pushed a wooden goblet of water into her hands. 'What happened?' he grunted.

Ally sipped the cool water, and then she began to tremble, suddenly realising just how close to death she had come. 'I was in the small library,' she said, looking at Paedur. She pulled the crumpled map out of her belt and laid it down on the table. 'The room where you showed me this map of the De Danann Isle.'

The bard nodded.

'I heard a noise at the window. It was Blade, with twelve vampir. They had climbed up the walls and broken a window. I knocked over some bookshelves to make a noise ...'

'We heard the sound,' Faolan said with a quick grin, 'we thought the whole floor was falling in.'

'But they would have got me if Megan hadn't arrived,' she finished, turning to look at the warrior-maid. 'How did you get here?' she asked, looking from Megan to Faolan and Colum.

'Paedur called us,' Colum said softly, his tiny voice barely above a whisper, his accent light and musical. His brown eyes were bright and sparkling. 'A magical call. I felt it in the earth...'

'And I heard it on the wind,' Faolan added. 'I created a wind-nathair and flew to Colum and then we sought Megan.'

The girl took up the story. 'I was already on my way here,' she explained. 'I had heard rumours that vampir and were-beasts had taken over Baddalaur, and I was coming to help my friends. I was fighting off a vampir family when Faolan and Colum arrived.' She smiled. 'One moment I was facing ten fanged vampir ... and the next the ground had opened and they had slithered down into a deep pit. I left them climbing out.'

'Your brother,' Faolan said suddenly, looking around, 'where's Ken?'

Ally swallowed, at a loss for words.

'Lost,' Ragallach grunted. 'Somewhere in the Desert of Bones, we think.'

'We must go for him,' the Windlord said immediately.

Paedur shook his head, his pale narrow face grim and unsmiling. 'We cannot.'

Everyone turned to look at him. 'I know he is lost and I, too, feel Ally's pain. But Ken is only one person, and we must now consider the future of the De Danann Isle.'

'Ken is our friend,' Colum said.

Megan nodded. She pushed back the leather band that kept

her hair from her forehead. 'In my tribe we consider friends to be a rare gift. Our families are not of our choosing, but we pick our own friends. We cannot abandon him.'

'We're not going to abandon him,' Paedur said patiently. 'And Ken is my friend too,' he reminded them. He sat down at the circular table and rested his hand and hook flat on the wood. His piercing dark eyes moved from face to face. 'We can go and look for Ken now if you wish,' he said. 'But before you make a decision,' he added quickly, 'think on this.' He took a deep breath. 'Many of Scathach's vampir army have left Baddalaur and taken to the roads. Megan met some on the way here. Everyone they meet they turn into vampir like themselves. This is like a stone dropped into a pond, ripples growing and spreading. Every day her army swells, and grows nearer to Falias. What will happen if a single vampir reaches the capital? There are perhaps ten thousand people there; merchants, soldiers, artisans, farmers, scholars. Think of it! Ten thousand vampir. Balor fought for many seasons to control the De Danann Isle, Scathach may do it in a single season.' He looked into Ally's troubled eyes. 'No-one will be safe. Scathach will control a vampir empire, and she will not be content with this single island. She will send her creatures out across the sea, to the lands to the west and east of here. And if we don't move against her now, then it will be too late. She will be too powerful.'

'I know that Paedur,' Ally said quietly. 'I come from your future; if you fail here, then the future is changed to some terrible vampir future ... and my time, my future, will have vanished. I will have nothing to return to.'

Paedur nodded. 'That is true.'

'But Ken is my brother, and I will not abandon him,' she said firmly. 'I think you should all go to Cichal on the Fomor Isles, as planned. Perhaps he will help. I'm going to the Desert of Bones to look for my brother.'

'Alone?' Paedur said, surprised.

'Alone,' she said.

'Not alone,' Ragallach grunted.

Dressed in grey leathers, wearing a long hooded riding cloak, Scathach walked alone through Baddalaur's empty streets. Two days ago they had been bustling with people, the narrow alley-ways crowded with merchants' stalls, selling everything from fruit to cloth. All the shops had been open, striped awnings covering the piled wares, the street, each with its particular trade — Silver Street, Gold Row, Pot Lane — loud with noise as the craftsmen worked in metal, wood or stone.

Now most of the shops were tightly sealed, windows barred and doors locked. Some remained open, but empty, doors swinging to and fro, banging in the breeze off the marshlands. The rotting remains of a tumbled fruit stall tainted the air with the stench of sweet decay and the place was filled with the droning of flies. The insects scattered as the Grey Warrior passed.

Scathach stopped in the square and looked up at the towering bulk of the College of Bards. Baddalaur the town had grown up around Baddalaur the College ... and the college had once been a fortress.

The Grey Warrior's cold eyes examined the towering build-ing, looking for any weaknesses. The building was ancient and had been created by a master craftsman who had designed it for defence. Towering walls completely encircled the college, and there were only two main gates, solid ironwood sandwiched between metal gates. As time had passed, additional wings and floors had been added to the original design, and houses had even been built right up against the walls — which was how Blade had managed to get into the building. He had first climbed onto a roof and then caught a hook on a lower window. Since the assassin's failed attack the previous day all the lower windows had been bricked up, and the guards on the walls had doubled. The defenders had dropped fire onto the houses that backed up against the walls, burning them to the ground.

Scathach knew she could assault Baddalaur, but that would take time, and she couldn't spare the time. Success was only possible if she moved swiftly. She could turn away, she knew that, she could set out for Falias at the head of a vampir army, and claim the capital as her own. But at the back of her mind there would always be the bard and his companions. If she couldn't capture them, she would have to destroy them. Because if she didn't destroy them then they would come for her, and they would do it for no other reason than they thought she was evil.

Scathach wasn't sure what evil was anymore, she wasn't even sure what she should call herself, though she knew what others called her: the Grey Warrior, Lady, Boabhan Sith, Vampir Queen. But she knew what the bard and his companions were: heroes. In every age, in every time, there were always heroes, men and women who stood against injustice simply because they thought it was wrong.

The Grey Warrior smiled, showing her razor teeth. Heroes had notoriously short lives.

The man and boy walked down the long smooth corridor in the place Ken had learned was called the Hive. 'What is your favourite colour?' Foltor asked suddenly.

'Red!' Ken said immediately.

'The colour of fire,' Foltor said with a smile, his teeth flashing whitely against his deeply tanned skin. 'Fire: the most dangerous of the elements, and also the deadliest of the elemental magics,' Foltor continued. He tucked his hands into the deep sleeves of his robe, and thrust his head forward, shoulders hunched. 'Scholars have long debated which is the most powerful of the magics: the windlore, the earthmagic, the firelore or the water mysteries. However, fire is one of the few elements that is almost completely destructive.'

Ken frowned. 'I'm not sure I agree,' he said cautiously.

Foltor smiled and glanced sidelong at the boy. 'What are its positive points?' he asked as they turned into a gently sloping passage that led upwards.

'Fire brings heat, and all human life needs heat to survive,' Ken said slowly, unsure if this was a test or not.

'Too much heat will kill,' the old man said.

The boy shrugged. 'But the complete absence of heat will kill also.'

'Not so. In the Ice-Fields beyond Thusal, communities live in the bitter cold.'

'But they still need heat to survive,' Ken said immediately. 'They need fire to cook their food and keep them warm at night.'

Foltor laughed softly. 'Just so. Good. You're not afraid to argue with me. And you're not afraid to think.' He stopped at the narrow slit window in the wall and gestured outside at the arid landscape. 'Look out here and tell me what you see.'

'A desert,' Ken said slowly, squinting against the harsh light. 'A stony desert.'

'A dead place?' Foltor asked, 'burnt barren by Nusas the sun?'

'No. There must be insects and reptiles and I've seen the dino... the Laghairt, the flying serpents.'

'There is life in the desert, but it is a harsh life, strong, deadly, savage, because it needs to be. The heat of Nusas has made it so.' He turned away from the window, one half of his face washed orange in the light, the other side in darkness. 'In the past some of the firelords have been like that desert life: fierce and savage. It is because the fire magic eats away inside them, changing them, altering them, burning them up. You must always guard against that happening. You must never give in to the lure of the fire magic.' He turned back to the desert. 'This place,' he said, gesturing to the rolling dunes, 'was once a green and fertile land ... until one of the previous firelords vented his anger on the place.' He glanced over his shoulder at Ken. 'That is your power.'

The boy stared at the bleak landscape. The desert looked as if it had existed for thousands of years, unchanged and unchanging and he couldn't imagine it covered in trees and grass, perhaps with a stream running through it.

'Five thousand people lived on this plain,' the priest said softly. 'They perished in an instant.' He suddenly turned away from the window and hurried down the corridor, as if eager to be away from the sight of the desert.

Ken hurried to catch up with him, sandals slapping off the stone.

'Once you open yourself up to the Firelore, it will burn in you like a fever, raging and uncontrollable. But when you feel the power threaten to burn out of control, remember the Desert of Bones ... and the five thousand lost souls whose ashes mingle with the sand.'

'I'll remember,' Ken promised. 'When do we begin training?'

'We already have,' Foltor said, almost sadly.

'Will it take me long to learn the firelore?'

'Not long,' the old man whispered. He stopped and caught Ken by the shoulders, turning him around so that they were looking at each other. 'Once I thought that I would be the firelord,' Foltor murmured. 'I was angry when I realised that it was not my destiny. Then, when I realised the awesome power and responsibility, I was relieved I had been spared that. I am sorry for you, Kenneth of the Clan Morand.' Reaching out, he placed the palm of his hand on top of Ken's skull.

A wave of heat flooded through the boy, lifting him up onto his toes, his arms flying out from his sides. Heat rolled in slow waves from the pit of his stomach, spreading down into his thighs and shins, into the soles of his feet, rolling upwards into his chest, through his shoulders and down into his hands. The intense heat sucked the air from his lungs, leaving him gasping for breath, sweat plastering his red hair to his skull, moisture curling along the sides of his face, running down his back. The beads of sweat suddenly sizzled into steam and then his clothing began to smoke where it touched his flesh, thin tendrils of grey smoke drifting up from his robe, curling out from the corners of his sandals. 'What's ... what's happening to me?' he gasped, his mouth parched and dry, his tongue swollen. He lifted his hands and looked at them; tiny blue flames were dancing along his finger-tips, smoke seeping out from beneath his nails.

'The Firelore cannot be taught,' Foltor said through gritted teeth as the flesh of his hands began to blacken and burn where it rested on Ken's head. 'It can only be released.' He suddenly pulled his hand back — as the boy erupted into a pillar of flame. 'Now, you are the Firelord!'

The world turned red.

Ken turned to Foltor, but he seemed to be looking at the priest through a shimmering liquid heat haze ... And then he realised what had happened ... what was happening.

He was on fire.

Ken opened his mouth to scream — and a stream of liquid fire splashed off the wall. He brought his hands to his face and watched the flames curl and twist from his fingers, balls of rolling fire gather in the palms of his hands. But he didn't feel any pain, only a dull heat and the sounds of distant roaring. The raging flames were dancing on his body, sparking from his flesh, but he didn't feel anything. When he rested his burning hand on the wall, it left a distinct black impression on the stone.

His fear vanished, and was replaced by wonder. He had seen magic worked in this world, had watched Faolan shape the wind and air, and Colum work the earth, he had ridden nathair and seen dinosaurs ... but this: this was magic. His magic!

Ken started to laugh then, cinders and sparks falling from his body, sizzling on the polished stone, blue-white flames dancing on his lips and tongue.

He had become the Firelord!

Suddenly the fire died to a sputtering crisp and the boy crumpled to the ground without a sound.

Foltor knelt beside the boy and reached out a hand. Ken's clothing had burnt away to scraps of charred cloth and his flesh was the colour and texture of coal. The priest could feel the heat radiating from the boy in long slow waves. Then Ken shuddered and his blackened skin cracked and split and fell away, revealing the pink flesh beneath.

Foltor bowed his head and breathed a quick prayer. The boy had survived: he was the true Firelord. 'The hardest part is over. Now you will learn to control this wild magic that rages through you. You must,' he said softly, 'for all our sakes.'

Ally hated the nathair: the feel of their dry, rasping flesh, the bitter-sour snake odour that seeped from their skins, the foul stench from their breath revolted her. And when their enormous yellow slit-pupilled eyes turned to look at her, she knew that she was looking at an intelligent alien creature that she could never understand. She understood Ragallach and Cichal the Fomor, even though they were non-human, because they were driven by the same wishes and desires as the human-kind. She had listened to Paedur telling the legend of the nathair, how they had once been angels who had rebelled against the gods in heaven and had been cast down and forced to wear the serpent's body. Looking at them, she could well believe it.

Ally jumped back as the nathair hissed at her, forked tongue flickering close to her face.

She had ridden the winged serpents before, sitting behind either Paedur or Ragallach, but now she would have to control one of the temperamental beasts herself.

'They fly towards the light,' Faolan said. 'It is the instinct they are born with. We control them by moving the flaps on the leather hoods that cover the top half of their head.' He held up what looked like an enormous leather bucket. 'Now, if you want the nathair to fly to the left, you would close down both eye pieces for a moment, then — *gently* — ease up the left eye covering. The nathair would immediately turn in that direction. However, if you do it too quickly, then the sudden burst of light will disorientate the creature and you might send it into a downward spiral.'

'And that's not good?' Ally asked.

'No,' Faolan said simply. 'If they fall too fast, with the lights confusing them, then they might not be able to spread their wings again. They would tumble and spin to the ground.' He saw the dismayed look on Ally's face and smiled reassuringly. 'Don't worry, that's not going to happen to you. But if it does,' he added quickly, 'simply close the eye patches for a few heartbeats, then allow a little light into the top of each. The nathair should immediately climb upwards.'

Ally swallowed hard. The nathair was staring at her, its eyes wide and unblinking: she was sure it knew what they were talking about.

'However,' Faolan continued, 'it is a day's ride to the Desert of Bones, and if you are delayed — bad weather for example — you must remember that the nathair do not usually fly at night, so you will have to land and find shelter.'

'But we've flown on the nathair at night,' Ally said.

'It is possible to trick them into flying, but that requires the hands of an experienced rider. And at night,' the Windlord added with a smile, 'Ragallach returns to his pig shape. Controlling the nathair and holding onto a pig would be too much to ask of any person.'

'Paedur showed me the route on the map,' Ally said quickly. 'We should be there by nightfall.'

'Remember also that the nathair don't like to fly over large bodies of water ...'

'... the reflections upset them,' Ally finished. 'There's only a couple of rivers between here and the Desert of Bones.'

'Well then, you're ready,' Faolan said, fitting the hood to the hissing serpent. It twisted its long neck and snapped at it, but he rapped it sharply on the nose and a colourless membrane moved across its yellow eyes, making it seem as if it blinked in surprise. 'Do you have everything?' he asked, reaching for the leather bags that hung on either side of the wooden saddle.

'I think so,' Ally said firmly, determined not to allow any fear to show in her voice.

'Everything except food,' Ragallach said, entering the chamber carrying a huge leather satchel. The boar-man was followed by Paedur, Megan and Colum.

Paedur stopped before Ally and looked her up and down, nodding approval.

'What are you smiling at?' the girl snapped.

Paedur shrugged. 'I was just thinking that when you're riding the nathair, wearing that black leather and with your red hair streaming out behind you, you're going to look like some creature out of a myth.'

'Megan gave me the clothes,' Ally said, feeling colour touch her cheeks. She wasn't used to compliments, but she had seen herself in the polished metal that passed for a mirror in this land, and she knew how spectacular she looked. She was wearing black leather trousers with a matching leather jerkin. High leather boots came up to her knees and she wore a stiff-collared leather riding-cape over her shoulders. Against the black leather, her red hair flamed dramatically.

'Is all in readiness?' Paedur asked, hard eyes narrowing as he looked over the nathair Faolan had chosen for her and Ragallach.

'We're ready,' the Torc Allta grunted.

'You know the plan,' Paedur said to Ragallach and Ally. 'You two will fly to the Desert of Bones. You have two days to find Ken. Meanwhile Megan, Faolan and I will head south to the Fomor Isles. Colum is remaining here to try to protect Baddalaur. We will all meet back here in three days time.'

The six friends gathered in a circle and looked at one another. They were all aware that this might be the last time they would see each other. Then Paedur stretched out his right hand, palm up, and Megan put her strong calloused hand into it. Ragallach added his hoof and Colum placed his small brown hand on top of that. Faolan's flesh looked pale against it and when Ally put her hand on top of that, Paedur placed his metal hook over the joined hands. They all felt the trickle of power that sparked from the metal. It coiled around their joined hands, curling blue and white up their arms, spinning around their chests.

'Whatever the future brings,' Paedur said softly, 'this moment will live within all of us. And while it lives, so do we.' He lifted his hook and the magic vanished.

Without a word, Ragallach lifted Ally onto the back of the enormous nathair, and climbed up behind her. Faolan mounted the second nathair and reached down to haul Paedur up behind him. Megan vaulted into the saddle behind Paedur.

'Three days,' Paedur called. 'We'll meet again. With Ken,' he added forcefully, smiling with a confidence he did not feel.

Ally turned away, unable to match his brave smile.

Shading her eyes against the early morning sun, Scathach watched as the two enormous nathair circled over Baddalaur's many towers and then split up, one heading south, the other moving off to the west. They were too high for her to make out any details, but she thought she saw the flash of the strange girl's red hair, and the glint of the bard's metal hook.

The Grey Warrior threw back her head and laughed, the sound echoing off the empty streets. She had won; they were fleeing. The warrior turned her cold eyes on Baddalaur. Before she marched on Falias, she was going to destroy the College, tear it down brick by brick, burn the library to the ground, turn the bards and scholars into vampir.

Scathach turned her back on Baddalaur. Massed in the shadows behind her were hundreds of her vampir army, red eyes glittering sharply. When night fell, she would unleash them on the College.

Ken was falling into the sun.

The huge yellow orb was rushing up at him, streamers of red and gold fire washing over him, bathing him in flames. Blue and white sparks danced about his head, spinning and tumbling, hissing where they touched his flesh. The white fire didn't burn; it felt like cool water where it splashed against his skin.

Stretching out his hand, he watched as long streamers of fire shot from his palm, individual flames dancing from each finger. He brought his hands together, concentrating the flames, shaping and moulding them like soft clay, into a fireball. Tossing the ball high, he watched it explode in mid-air, raining down streamers of multi-coloured fire.

The boy threw back his head and laughed ... and the flames roared higher.

Then the sun went out.

~

Ken opened his eyes and groaned aloud. Every muscle in his body ached and throbbed and he was shivering slightly. He blinked in the dim light, trying to make out details of his surroundings.

'Don't move.'

He recognised Foltor's voice, coming from across the room.

He licked dry lips and attempted to speak. 'Don't speak.'

Cloth rasped and he was aware that the priest was approaching. A strong hand gripped the back of his head, lifting him, the narrow mouth of a flask pressed against his lips. Bitter water trickled against the back of his throat.

'Listen to me,' Foltor said from the shadows. 'I have released the fire-magic within you. While your body adjusts to the changes as the power moves through your flesh and bones you must remain in cool darkness. The touch of warm sunlight on your skin would bring the flames boiling to the surface.'

The boy nodded. He wondered how long he'd slept.

'You have slept for the entire day, and you have been dreaming about fire.'

Ken wondered how he knew.

'How do I know?' Foltor asked. 'Twice you reached out and shot streamers of flame around the room, once your entire body was engulfed in intense blue fire, another time sparks spun around your body like circling stars.' The priest took a deep breath. 'This is the most dangerous time for you, Ken. If you do not learn to control the fire then it will burn you up. But the Firelore can be tamed: the flames will flare when you are angry or upset, when you are frightened. And when the ancient magic has poured through you, it will leave you weakened and exhausted. I can teach you how to control your breath, how to visualise the fire flowing from your finger tips, how to shape the fireballs, but only you can learn how to master your temper, your fear.' Foltor sighed. 'Training a Firelord should take ten seasons ... we have days.'

Ally jerked awake, eyes wide and staring. She immediately squeezed them shut again as the blazing sunlight blinded her.

She had been dreaming about Ken. Her brother had been standing in the midst of a whirling circle of fire, face and arms turned to the sky, red hair streaming upwards. Sparks spiralled from his clothes of liquid fire. In the dream she had been trapped outside the circle, the intense flames kept beating her back every time she tried to get to Ken. She had awoken as the flames had risen up in a huge fiery wave and washed over her.

It took her a few moments to orientate herself. She was sitting on the back of the nathair, behind Ragallach. Her arms were wrapped around the Torc Allta's waist and her belt was tied securely to the saddle. Her long red hair streamed out behind her in the warm, scented breeze.

Ragallach felt the girl awaken and twisted his huge head to look at her. His tiny pink pig eyes were filled with concern. 'You slept,' he said, a statement rather than a question.

'I must have dozed off after we ate,' Ally agreed.

She had guided the nathair for most of the morning, experimenting with the hoods until she was confident she could control the flying serpent. Shortly before noon, she had brought the creature down in a great swooping circle to land on a gently sloping hillside. She and Ragallach had eaten dried fruits and drunk some of the tepid water from their flasks before taking to the air again, this time with the Torc Allta controlling the nathair.

'You were dreaming,' Ragallach continued.

'How do you know?' she wondered.

'You were moaning softly as if you were in pain. You were dreaming about your brother?'

Ally nodded. 'He was trapped in a circle of fire and I couldn't get to him,' she said softly.

'This heat makes you think of fire,' Ragallach grunted. He jerked his head upwards to where the sun shone in a cloudless sky. Close to the horizon the sky was a pale delicate blue, but overhead it was almost white, bleached of all colour.

'We've reached the desert already?' Ally shifted in the saddle to look down. Directly below, the landscape was a wasteland of rock and stone that stretched on into the distance. At first glance she thought it was a uniform brown colour, but as she stared at it, she realised she could make out a hundred different shades of red and bronze, gold and orange.

'The Western Desert,' Ragallach said, 'sometimes known as the Desert of Bones.'

Ally looked left and right across the wasteland and felt despair wash over her: Ken could be anywhere in this vast area. She felt tears sting her eyes. 'I'm never going to find him, am I, Ragallach?'

'You will find him,' the Torc Allta said firmly. 'You have to believe that you will find him — you must believe it. We know he is here. Allow your instincts to lead you to him. Besides,' he added with a terrifying grin that showed his savage teeth, 'we know that he must be somewhere to the south and west of here, close to the Cliffs of Laghairt Dis ... the Serpent's Hell,' he translated.

Ally followed the Torc Allta's pointing arm. 'How do we know Ken's there?' she wondered.

'Before we set out, Paedur studied the latest reports from the bards and scholars returning to Baddalaur. A scholar returning from Breccan Mor, the city at the edge of the desert, had heard a rumour of a red-haired boy held captive by the Silent Ones.' Ragallach smiled again. 'The Silent Ones worship fire!' he added triumphantly.

'And I dreamed of fire,' Ally whispered.

'It's a place to start,' Ragallach said. He adjusted the reins, lowering the right eye patch over the nathair's head, raising the left slightly, bringing the serpent around in a slow gentle curve.

'What do we know about the Silent Ones?' Ally shouted above the crack of the wind.

'Very little,' Ragallach said. 'They never speak except to raise their voices in prayer. They are supposed to worship the element of fire in all its manifestations, including worshipping the sun,' he added.

Ally heard the strange note in his voice. 'What's wrong?' she demanded. 'What are you not telling me?'

The Torc Allta said nothing, concentrating on controlling the serpent. 'It's something to do with the Silent Ones, isn't it? Something to do with their sun worship. Ragallach — tell me,' she insisted, pounding on his hairy shoulder with her fist.

'The Silent Ones are supposed to offer sacrifice to the Nusas, the Sun,' the Torc Allta said simply.

Sacrifice.

Ally mouthed the word. She remembered reading about the Aztecs — or was it the Maya? — who worshipped the sun, and killed thousands of people on top of their stepped pyramids, offering their hearts to the sun.

And even though the day was blistering hot, Ally felt the touch of ice on her spine and in the pit of her stomach.

Sacrifice.

The girl shivered.

~

Nusas blazed too bright, too warm.

Ragallach hated the bright sunlight. It hurt his sensitive eyes, dried his moist snout, and burned his pink skin. He glanced up into the heavens, gauging the time. Early afternoon; he wondered how much sunshine was left. If they were going to fly in this blistering sunshine again tomorrow, he was going to have to rig up some sort of cover. Twisting in the high saddle, the Torc Allta looked at Ally. The intense heat had exhausted her and she was dozing again. The red-haired girl's pale skin was red and blotched, her forehead shining with sunburn.

He would have to find some place to land and treat the sunburn before it got worse. Leaning over the edge of the nathair, he peered down, snout wrinkling, tasting the odours on the hot air. Catching the faintest hint of water, he concentrated on that smell, eliminating all others — the acrid odour of the sands, the metallic tang of burnt rock, the stench of the nathair, his own meaty smell, Ally's more delicate odour — until he had located the source of the smell. Adjusting the reins, he turned the nathair towards the south. Squinting hard through the shimmering landscape, he saw a black dot on the horizon. Shading his small eyes with his hoof, he saw the shape grow into a small stand of trees. Ragallach grunted. Trees meant water, and water meant mud and a moist mud-pack would ease the pain of sunburn.

~

Ally opened her eyes as the nathair came to a halt in a cloud of sand. She looked around in confusion, wondering why they'd stopped ... and where?

'Oasis,' Ragallach said, sliding stiffly out of the saddle, reaching up to lift the girl down. Her legs buckled as she touched the ground and the Torc Allta held her until feeling returned to her numb feet. Clinging to the creature as pins and needles tingled in her toes, Ally looked around. They were at the edge of a small stand of enormous gnarled palm trees, situated in a shallow hollow in the desert. She could see the metallic blue-white sparkle of water through the trees and suddenly realised just how hot and dry she felt.

'Don't drink the water,' Ragallach warned.

Ally grinned — he sounded just like her mother when they went on holidays to Spain — and then she frowned as her dried lips split. Bringing her hands to her face, she touched warm cheeks, roasting forehead and a nose that was almost too hot to touch. 'Sunburn,' she mumbled through cracked lips. She looked at the Torc Allta and realised that he wasn't much better. Ragallach's pink skin was a deep angry red and his snout was as cracked and as dry as her lips.

Standing back, she watched as the Torc Allta drove a pointed stake into the sand and looped the nathair's reins around it. The flying serpent was restless in the heat, its flat head turning to hiss at Ragallach, forked tongue flickering. The boar-man rapped it across the nose with his hoof, and the nathair drew back its head in quick surprise. Ragallach pulled the hood down over its head, blinding it, and the nathair fell asleep.

Ally followed Ragallach into the shade of the trees, immediately grateful for the shadows. Her skin prickled uncomfortably and she knew it would start to peel soon, just like that time in Spain when her skin came off in paper-thin sheets ...

'You're smiling,' Ragallach said.

'I was thinking I should have brought some sun tan lotion.'

The Torc Allta frowned. 'Sun tan lotion?'

'A special cream that humans in my time smear on their skins to prevent the sun from burning them.'

Ragallach nodded. 'We have that here.'

Ally looked at him in surprise. 'You have?'

The Torc Allta knelt by the edge of the irregular pool of glistening water and dug his paw into the soft margin, dragging up a thick globule of dripping mud.

Ally looked at him blankly.

Ragallach started smearing the liquid mud on his face and arms.

'You cannot be serious,' the girl whispered. 'Well you're not getting me to put that on ...' she continued.

And then the nathair started screaming.

Faolan brought the enormous nathair around the Fomor Isles in a long slow circle, giving the guards in their tall towers plenty of time to report in. Angling off to the left, he flew low over the Forest of Caesir, the tips of the serpent's wings touching the tree tops, scattering leaves, sending birds flapping upwards in screeching disarray, before he finally brought the creature down onto the ancient stone bridge that joined the Fomor Isles to the mainland. The centre section of the bridge was missing; the Fomor would lower it in place when they went raiding into the dark forest, or marched on the human-kind cities.

'Have we made enough noise?' the Windlord asked. He had to raise his voice above the screeches and howls coming from the disturbed birds and animals in the forest behind them.

Megan grinned. 'The whole forest knows we're here.'

'But more importantly, the Fomor also know we're here,' Paedur added.

Leaving Faolan on the back of the nathair, Paedur and Megan dismounted and walked right up to the edge of the bridge. Directly below them the water curled dark and red, bubbling with what looked like a swirling oily stain. The stain was actually composed of millions of tiny ravenous organisms that fed off all living matter — animal, vegetable or human — and was capable of stripping flesh to the bone in a matter of heartbeats. The Fomor dumped their refuse into the water to keep the stain in place: it ensured that the Gor Allta, the Beast Folk, and the Fomor's mortal enemies, who inhabited the ancient forest couldn't swim across and attack the island. Not even their wooden boats were safe from the red stain's voracious appetite.

Megan nudged a piece of wood with the toe of her boot and watched it tumble out over the edge and spiral into the water below. It disappeared without a sound. She remembered the last time they had come to the Fomor Isle. They had rowed out from the mainland in a boat coated with a liquid that was supposed to repel the red stain. They had been less than half way across when the first leaks began, and had barely made it to the other side before the boat had been consumed.

'Fomor,' Paedur's voice was low and calm.

Megan looked up as a trio of Fomor guards raced out from the cave mouth that marked the entrance to the warren of caves where the Fomor lived. They took up positions on the edge of their side of the bridge. Their serpent's tongues were flickering nervously, sunlight running coldly off the long stone swords two clutched in taloned claws. The third beast was cradling a heavy wooden crossbow.

'Tell Cichal we wish to see him,' Paedur said immediately, using his trained bardic voice. The powerful sound echoed off the water and rang off the stone cliffs behind the Fomor. Although their faces betrayed no expressions, they were clearly astonished at the demand, tongues and tails flicking madly. One raised his heavy cross-bow and sighted the bard. 'Don't be stupid,' Paedur said easily. 'Don't you know who we are?'

The Fomor pulled the trigger and the stone-tipped crossbow bolt hissed through the air towards the young bard's chest ...

... And stopped a finger's breadth from his skin.

The bolt hung suspended in mid-air, trembling slightly, vibrating softly, then it abruptly flipped around and darted back towards the Fomor who had fired the shot. He managed a single hiss of surprise before the bolt struck the crossbow from his grasp, shattering the trigger mechanism.

Megan glanced over her shoulder in time to see the Windlord drop his hand, a smile on his lips.

'This is Megan, the Warrior-Maid,' Paedur continued as if nothing had happened. He raised his left arm, sunlight glistening off his hook and indicated the golden-haired boy on the nathair, 'And you have just had an example of the Windlord's power ...'

'And you are Paedur the Bard.'

The voice was a low grating grumble, and the three guards turned as another Fomor appeared from the shadows of the cave mouth behind them. They immediately bowed deeply and stood back. The Fomor was far bigger and broader than the others, his scaled skin bearing the many lines of old scars, and he wore a metallic patch over his left eye. The hilt of an enormous stone sword protruded over his left shoulder.

'Very little the human-kind does surprises me,' the Fomor continued, walking up the bridge, clawed toes out over the edge of the precipice. His tail twitched and curled around his left foot. 'However, finding you here astonishes me.'

'I'm a bit surprised myself,' Paedur admitted. 'I never thought I'd see you again, Cichal of the Fomor.'

'Tell me why I shouldn't order my troops to cut you down,' he hissed. 'You cannot turn aside all our arrows and spears.'

Paedur smiled. He held up his right hand and extended two fingers. 'Two reasons. First because you are a creature of honour. You have proven that time and again. We present no threat to you, so you will not order your Troop to fire on us. Secondly, because you're curious. You're wondering what we're doing here.'

'It would be a mistake to give the Fomor human characteristics and emotions,' Cichal snapped, tail curling and uncurling angrily.

'But I think I know enough about the Fomor species to know that you must be curious,' the bard said quietly, 'otherwise you would not survive as a species. The greatest inventions, the latest discoveries are made by the curious.'

Cichal sighed. 'Your presence here intrigues me. What do you want?'

'Your help.'

Cichal's laughter was a huge rolling hiss.

~

Megan was nervous. She kept touching the slender dagger she wore taped to the inside of her left arm. She knew it wouldn't do much against the thick hide of the Fomor, but she took some comfort from the fact that she wasn't entirely defenceless.

Taking a deep breath, the warrior-maid looked around the enormous cave. She had never seen so many Fomor gathered together in one place. She saw females and young, the children looking half-formed, more serpentine than their parents, the females finer boned, with splashes of colour on the scales around their eyes and throat.

And the smell was indescribable.

Megan glanced sidelong at Paedur. He was sitting cross-legged on a beautifully woven mat, hook and hand folded into his lap, his face calm and expressionless. Faolan sat behind Paedur directly across from Megan. The Windlord's hands were closed into tight fists, but she could see that the veins in his neck were taut: sure signs that he was nervous. Nervous? Megan felt a smile curl her lips. She wasn't nervous. She was terrified.

They had been taken across the bridge once the centre section had been lowered into place, onto the Fomor Isles. Cichal had silently stretched out his enormous claws and the bard had placed his boot knife into it. Faolan's knife had followed, and then Megan's two knives, her throwing stars, blow-pipe and boomerang. When he was convinced that they had no more weapons to hand over, he had turned away and they had followed him into the shadowy cave mouth. The entrance to the cave had been decorated and carved to resemble the head of a snarling Fomor. Megan shivered: it looked as if they were walking into its mouth.

The three companions had followed Cichal down through the winding, twisting tunnels. News of their arrival had spread and the corridors were lined with hundreds of silent Fomor, yellow eyes glowing in the dim light. When they passed, the hissing would begin: the sounds of reptilian whispers.

Cichal had finally led them into a chamber, deep in the heart of the isle. The cave was enormous. Circular windows threw slanting sunbeams onto the floor of the chamber, vaguely illuminating the tattered banners and flags on the walls. Weapons, from the crudest stone axes to the most up-to-date spears and crossbows, hung on the walls. Dominating the centre of the floor was an enormous and elaborate throne made from thick yellow bones.

As the chamber began filling with Fomor, two young warriors appeared and spread three mats on the floor before the throne. 'Sit,' Cichal hissed, the only words he had spoken since they had stepped onto the island. When they had settled onto the mats, the Fomor had turned and walked away.

They had been sitting there for what seemed like a long time when Megan leaned across to Paedur and whispered, her breath warm on his ear. 'What are we waiting for?'

'Morc the Pitiless,' Paedur breathed, 'the King of the Isle.'

Even as he was speaking, doors boomed in the distance and a ripple ran through the assembled Fomor. Guards snapped to attention, others bowing low, some even dropping to the floor.

More doors opened, closer this time, and a draft of warm foul air washed across the three humans.

Megan resisted the temptation to turn around. She had encountered Morc once before, when she and Ken and Ally had been captured. He was one of the most terrifying creatures she had ever encountered. He was taller, broader, uglier, more serpentine than any of the other Fomor. He was also reputed to be a thousand years old, having been granted immortality by a sorcerer in an age when the Fomor ruled the world.

The warrior-maid glanced at Paedur, hoping he knew what he was doing. The last time she had stood before the savage Fomor King he had wanted to eat her. Morc had lived in an age when humans were raised and hunted for food.

The musty odour of snake suddenly filled her nostrils as Morc neared. The hem of his embroidered cloak actually brushed her hair as he passed, sending a shudder down her spine. Before the Fomor settled into his bone throne, his rasping voice boomed out, echoing off the walls. 'Tell me why I shouldn't feast off human flesh?'

The nathair's cry sliced through the dry desert air. It was like a child's scream — high-pitched and terrible.

Crouching at the water's edge Ally froze, the sound shocking her motionless, but Ragallach turned and raced back towards the flying serpent. Ally came slowly to her feet, turning to follow the Torc Allta. She caught glimpses of him through the trees ... then she heard him squeal with a mixture of fright and pain. The sound galvanised her into action and she raced after him, bursting out of the concealment of the trees close to where they had tied down the nathair.

And stopped.

Two enormous bird-like creatures were circling the tethered serpent, pecking at it with narrow pointed beaks, their gaping mouths filled with hundreds of bloody teeth. The hooded nathair was screaming and twisting, lashing out blindly with tail and wings, snapping at the empty air with its savage teeth. A bird snapped at the serpent's head, but the leather mask protected the nathair's eyes, and its sinuous tail arced high over its body, catching the bird across its breast. It crumpled to the ground in a flurry of paper-thin wings.

Ragallach.

Where was Ragallach?

Feeling sick to her stomach, Ally crept closer. The dry desert air was foul with the stench of the nathair and a musty bird-like odour from the remaining creature ... and then the girl abruptly recognised it. She had a picture of it in one of her school books: it looked like a pterodactyl. But the pterodactyls had become extinct millions of years ago ...

And Ally suddenly realised just how far into the past she and her brother had travelled. They had often talked about it, wondering how far back they'd gone, speculating that they had travelled maybe three or four thousand years into the past. But now she knew that they had gone back much further than that.

The pterodactyl swooped in, jaws snapping and the nathair's thin green blood spurted.

Ragallach. Where was he?

A splash of colour almost directly beneath the injured nathair caught her attention. Shading her eyes with her hand, she squinted hard, trying to identify the shape ... and suddenly realised that it was the Torc Allta lying motionless on the ground. As she watched the nathair's razor-tipped claw rose and fell inches from Ragallach's outstretched arm. Ally looked up in alarm: if the savage bird-creature kept driving the nathair back, it would stand on Ragallach.

Without thinking Ally darted forward, eyes fixed on the fighting nathair and pterodactyl. They were intent on one another, but all they had to do was to turn and they would see her. A single blow of wing or claw or the snap of a jaw could kill her.

Was that what had happened to Ragallach?

Crouching low, Ally dashed forward, caught one of the Torc Allta's enormous legs and pulled hard, attempting to drag him back. He didn't budge.

The nathair's tail whipped around, hissing through the air in front of the pterodactyl, crashing back to earth close enough to shower the girl with sand. The hind foot rose, fell, rose again, pounding deep into the sand close to Ragallach's ears.

Ally bit her lips to prevent herself from screaming aloud. Catching the Torc Allta's hoof, she dug in her heels and dragged with all her might. For a moment nothing happened, then Ragallach slid backwards — just as the nathair's claw pounded into the ground where Ragallach's head had lain.

As the fight between the two creatures increased in ferocity, Ally slowly dragged Ragallach away. The Torc Allta was incredibly heavy; her heart was pounding in her chest, coloured spots danced before her eyes and the muscles of her legs, arms and shoulders ached with the agony of the effort. But the screaming, slashing, roaring, hissing battle spurred her on until she reached the shelter of the sand dunes close to the edge of the oasis. When she could not longer see the beasts, she stopped and turned the Torc Allta over to look at him. There was an ugly bruise across the top of his head and he was coated from head to hoof in sand, but otherwise he seemed unhurt. Laying her head on his broad hairy chest, she listened intently for the pounding of his heartbeat. It thumped solidly beneath her ear.

'I'm alive.'

Ally sat back, blinking quickly to hide the tears of relief.

Ragallach sat up stiffly, pressing a paw to his bruised forehead. 'I walked into the nathair's tail,' he groaned.

'Luckily you've a thick skull,' Ally smiled shakily.

'No,' the Torc Allta whispered, reaching out for Ally's hand, 'luckily I have a friend like you.'

On the far side of the sand dunes the screaming and hissing of the battling creatures rose to a terrible crescendo ... then abruptly stopped.

Later, much later, the flies came.

Blade the Assassin stood in the shadows and watched the sun dip
lower in the heavens. There wasn't much time left. When the sun
went down, Scathach had ordered him to attack Baddalaur —
and burn it to the ground!

The assassin shifted uncomfortably, shivering in the early
evening chill. Burning Baddalaur was never part of his plan. He
had grown up in this town, and though he followed a life of crime,
he had always had the greatest of respect and admiration for
Baddalaur's monks and scholars. When he had been very young,
he had been living rough on the streets, scavenging food from
the rubbish tips, sipping water from puddles in the gutter. One
day he had been found by one of the grey-robed monks, who had
taken him to an orphanage run by the monks and scholars of
Baddalaur. They had taken him in without question, fed and
clothed him and given him a warm bed. He'd been expecting
them to throw him out onto the street the following morning, but
no-one had asked him to leave. In the days and months that
followed, he had joined the small classes, and learned simple
words and numbers. The brothers had asked nothing in return.
When he eventually left the orphanage nearly three years later,
it was only because he had grown bored by the safe life behind
the college walls. In that time he had come to know the monks
and scholars. He knew they harmed no-one. They were not
warriors, they never took sides in disputes, and they often acted

as judges and peacemakers. They spent their time collecting the history, lore and legends of the De Danann Isles, keeping alive the stories of the past, adding the tales to the Great Library of Baddalaur, which was considered one of the marvels of the known world.

And now Scathach wanted to burn the library to the ground — to destroy the vast collection of books, maps and charts. In one move, she would erase the results of a thousand years of collected knowledge.

'I will plunge this world into ignorance,' she had boasted earlier. 'I will burn all the books, I will forbid writing and teaching, ban the learning of history. I will keep the people ignorant. Ignorant people are easily controlled.'

Blade raised his head to look at the college's solid walls. All the doors and the lower windows were barred, but he had no doubts that he could lead a troop of the newly formed vampir knights into the college. Then they could fight their way to the gates and open them to the awaiting vampir army. Before dawn, the entire community of monks, scholars and bards and the people who had fled to the safety of the college walls would have fallen victim to the vampir's sharp teeth.

The assassin raised his fingers to touch the metal and stone collar around his neck which Scathach claimed prevented him from turning into a Torc Allta. Blade wondered how long he could remain useful to the Grey Warrior. In the college there were men of education and power, men who had studied the arts of war down through the ages, warrior-bards who could train her vampir army, gifted craftsmen who could shape metal into armour and weapons.

What use would she have for a simple assassin when she had access to these men and their combined knowledge?

Blade's short stubby fingers ran across the collar again, touching rough stone and smooth metal. When he took a deep breath, he felt the collar tighten around his neck, almost as if it was choking him. He wanted to pull the collar off, but the Grey Warrior insisted that only she knew the spell that prevented the Torc Allta's bite from turning him into a were-beast.

But what if she was lying?

The sudden thought struck him like a blow. What if she was lying? Hadn't she told him she wanted to keep people ignorant, because ignorant people were easily controlled. Did she consider him ignorant ... or was she simply lying about the collar to keep him under control? She could always turn him into a vampir, couldn't she? ... No. Blade shook his head. He had noticed that Scathach's vampir had no will of their own. They did what they were told and no more. The Grey Warrior would always need a few human-kind to help her control her army ... but that meant she would need some method of controlling those humans.

Blade touched the collar. He knew how he was controlled; without the collar she would have no further hold over him. He looked up at the college, his dark eyes seeking out the hospital windows. Those scholars and bards who had dedicated their lives to healing practised their arts there. Maybe Scathach wasn't the only person who knew the cure, maybe one of the healers in the college would know a cure for the disease, or at least how to keep it at bay.

But if he attacked the college, destroyed the books and the learned bards were turned into vampir, he would never find a cure and he would be a slave to the Grey Warrior for the rest of his life ... and he guessed that that would be very short indeed.

Blade's grip tightened on the collar and with a savage twist he pulled it off. Now he *had* to warn the college ... and pray that they knew a cure.

'If you kill us,' Paedur said loudly, 'you will have condemned the Fomor race to extinction.'

No sound broke the long silence that followed.

Morc leaned forward in his bone chair, long narrow claws tapping the smoothly polished ivory arms. His yellow eyes fixed unblinkingly on the bard, forked tongue flickering slowly. When he finally spoke, his voice was a low, rasping rumble.

'Would you lie to me, human-kind?'

Paedur stared at him. 'I am a bard,' he said proudly. 'I do not lie!'

'You are a storyteller,' Morc snapped. 'Storytellers are liars! Would you lie to me?' he asked again.

'Why would I lie to you?' Paedur said simply.

The ancient lizard opened his mouth to reply ... and then closed it again. He couldn't think of an answer. Finally, he said, 'Why are you here?'

'To ask for your help.' Paedur kept his eyes fixed on Morc. He knew that the next few moments would decide not only the future of the De Danann Isle but also the future of the known world. If he and his companions failed here today, then Scathach would win and her vampir would claim the earth.

Morc twisted around in the bone throne to look at Cichal. He spoke quickly in the Fomor tongue, a mixture of rapid hissing sounds and clicks which the human throat was incapable of duplicating and which went beyond human hearing. 'This is a trick?' he asked.

Cichal's tongue flickered. 'I do not think so. I have gone up against these human-kind before. They are wily, but not without honour.'

'They destroyed Balor,' Morc reminded him.

'Balor destroyed himself,' Cichal said quickly, 'though it is true that these human-kind were instrumental in his downfall.' A colourless membrane moved across his single eye and the corners of his terrifying mouth moved in what might have been mistaken for a smile. 'But if Balor had not been destroyed, then we would have been forced to move against him ourselves. That would have led us in a destructive battle with the human-kind. Many of the Fomor would been slain in such a confrontation. By defeating him, these human whelps saved many Fomor lives.'

Morc sat back into his throne, which creaked beneath the weight. 'You sound as if you admire them.'

'There is much to admire in them,' Cichal admitted.

'Are you saying I should listen to them?'

'Yes,' Cichal said simply. 'Listen to them ... afterwards you can decide whether to eat them or not.'

Morc turned back to the humans. He glared at them, his massive head shifting to look at each in turn: the hard-eyed warrior maid, the assured confidence of the Windlord, the expressionless mask of the bard. His tongue flickered, tasting the air, scenting their fear. The scent of fear decided him; they had come here to face him even though they were frightened. That took great courage. 'Know this,' he said suddenly, rising to his feet, towering above them, 'if you lie to me, or attempt to trick me, I will have you coated in honey, roasted over a slow fire, then I will tear you apart and feast off your flesh. Follow me,' he hissed, and turned and strode away, his thick tail slithering across the floor behind him.

'I think I've gone off honey,' Megan muttered as they followed the Fomor king deeper into the warren of caves.

~

After the gloom of the endless corridors which were illuminated by a dim fungal light, the sudden shaft of sunlight made the three humans throw up their hands to cover their eyes. Morc and Cichal were unaffected, an inner eyelid automatically sliding down to protect their eyes.

Morc had led them out onto a balcony set high into the mountainside that looked out over the heart of the Fomor Isle. There was no rail between the edge of the balcony and the long fall onto the forest floor far below.

Faolan, who had no fear of heights, walked right up to the edge of the balcony and looked out across the island, towards the sparkling sea. He noticed that while much of the isle was covered by dense trees, the interior was laid out in a series of long regular groves. Pointing a slender finger, he turned his head to look at Morc, 'Are those the famous Fomor grape groves?'

Morc took a deep breath, seeming to swell with pride. 'Those groves are part of my own estates. Is Fomor wine well known amongst your people?' he asked casually.

'Fomor wine is considered the best in the world,' Faolan said immediately, 'especially the variety known as Serpent's Tail.' He lifted up his left hand, forming a ring with thumb and index finger. 'The fat clay flasks bear an imprint of a snake swallowing its own tail. That is my father's favourite, and he is considered an expert,' he added.

Morc's teeth flashed briefly and his tongue flickered. 'Serpent's Tail is my own blend,' he hissed.

Cichal gave a short angry hiss, and the Fomor king suddenly remembered where he was. 'Now, tell me what you have come here to say,' he snapped, 'and remember — no lies.'

Paedur folded his arms across his chest and leaned back against the warm stone of the cliff face. Sunlight turned his pale skin the colour of parchment and blazed off the metal hook that rested against the dark material of his jerkin.

'There is a vampir abroad on the De Danann Isle,' he said simply. 'A Baobhan Sith,' he added.

Morc made a peculiar sinuous movement with his right hand and stepped back from the young man. His tongue was dancing madly. 'A Baobhan Sith,' he spat. He made the waving shape in the air again with right claw, tracing a magical symbol to ward off evil.

Paedur blinked in surprise. 'You know what a Baobhan Sith is?'

'You forget that I am old, old, old, human-kind. As you measure time, I have walked this world for a thousand years and more. I know about the vampir and especially the Baobhan Sith, the Vampir Queens.' Then he suddenly shook his head. 'Now I know this is a trick. The last of the Sith disappeared generations ago.'

'Well one has reappeared,' Paedur said firmly. 'Already she has taken over Baddalaur and turned its citizens into blood-sucking slaves.'

Cichal leaned forward. 'Does this creature have a name?'

Paedur's smile was icy. 'She has — and it is a name you will recognise. Scathach.'

'The Grey Warrior!' Cichal hissed. He started to shake his head, but suddenly stopped. 'It starts to make sense now. A grey warrior, with teeth filed to points ... and I never saw her eat food or drink wine.' He turned to Morc. 'Vampir are described as being grey, with filed teeth. And they never eat because they find their sustenance in blood.'

'Scathach,' Morc rumbled. 'I remember there was a creature of the Sith with that name, but a long time ago ...'

Cichal spoke quickly to the king in the Fomor tongue, describing Scathach. Morc's huge head nodded slowly. 'It is her ... it must be.' He turned to look at Paedur. 'Why have you come here with this news?'

'I've already told you and Cichal too. We — the human-kind — need your help.'

The two Fomor looked at him, their serpentine faces unreadable.

'Scathach has raised a vampir army, but an army of humans,' Paedur continued. 'As far as we know there are no Fomor amongst them. These human vampir will easily defeat other humans; all they have to do is to bite. But human teeth will not penetrate Fomor hide or armour.' The young bard took a deep breath. 'I have come here to ask you to send a Fomor army to stand against Scathach's vampir army, until we find a way to defeat her.'

The Fomor continued to stare at him.

Faolan took up a position to one side of the bard, Megan on the other. 'I have no powers to see into the future,' Paedur added, 'but I think I can tell you what will happen. When Scathach has changed all the humans into vampir, she will turn her attentions to the were-beasts and the non-humans. And those she cannot make into vampir she will kill.' Paedur stopped. There was nothing more he could say. Now it was up to Morc.

'Not even a vampir army could defeat us,' Cichal said proudly.

The bard shook his head. 'Not even the mighty Fomor could stand against the entire De Danann Isle. And remember, as she turns humans into vampir, she will be taking control of generals and magicians, bards, scholars, doctors, warriors. Think of all their skills ranged against you.'

'The human-kind is correct,' Morc rumbled, 'we could not stand against them all.' The Fomor king turned away and looked across the island, claws clasped behind his back, head sunk onto his chest. 'Once, a long time ago,' he said very softly, 'I led my people against a Baobhan Sith vampir queen. She fought at the head of a huge army of black-skinned men from the land to the east of here. They were fearsome warriors,' he added, shaking his head in memory. 'I lost many of my clan, including two of my sons. One fell in battle as he fought to defend me, the other ... One night I awoke to find a sword at my throat. I struck out blindly, felling my attacker ... but when the lantern was lit, I discovered that I had slain my own son.' Morc shook his head. 'But no, he was not my son then, he had been turned into a vampir by the Baobhan Sith herself: the first — and only — Fomor vampir.'

The king dipped his head slightly, turning to look at Cichal and hissed a question at him.

The Fomor warrior chose to answer in the language the three

humans could understand. 'I can have ten full Troops ready to march before the day is out.'

Morc spun around. His claw stabbed the air between them. 'I will grant you your request. But not because you have asked me, and not to save the human-kind, or the De Danann Isle, or even the Fomor people. I will grant you your request to avenge my son.' Then, clasping his hands behind his back again, he turned to the island and the distant grape groves.

As Cichal led the humans away, Morc raised his head. 'And when we attack this Scathach Baobhan Sith, I will lead the Troops myself.'

The oasis came alive at night. In the solid darkness, hissing, creaking, crackling, coughing, roaring, squawking sounds appeared all around as the night creatures came down to the water to drink, or to feast off the dead nathair and the two dead pterodactyls.

Ally sat in the tree and clutched the small pig tightly and prayed that none of the shapes that moved below her were capable of climbing.

Now that night had fallen, her sunburn had started tingling painfully, the muscles she had wrenched pulling Ragallach away from the nathair were aching, her numerous scratches and bruises were stinging and she was hungry. Almost unnoticed, tears rolled down her cheeks. Feeling moisture splash onto her hands, she angrily brushed the tears away. She wasn't going to give in to tears.

Taking a deep breath, she tried to take stock of the situation, but she had to admit that it didn't look good. She and Ragallach were lost in the desert, without food or water. They were at least half a day's journey by nathair from her brother's last known location, but it would take three days to walk that distance ... and they couldn't set out across the blistering desert without food or water. Nor could they stay here. Ragallach had shown her the dozens of different tracks embedded in the soft mud around the edge of the pool and named the creatures. Some of the beasts he had described sounded terrifying.

So what were they going to do?

She didn't know.

Tilting her head back against the rough bark of the tree, Ally squeezed her eyes shut. This time she couldn't stop the tears from flowing.

Ken.

Where are you Ken?

Where are you!

~

Ken sat bolt upright, coming awake with a scream that sent a sizzling fireball across the room to splash against the stonework.

A cold damp cloth was placed against his forehead, hissing and steaming against his blistering skin, forcing his head back onto the stone pillow.

'What is it?' The voice was vague, distant, like a half-remembered dream. 'What did you see?'

'Ally,' he mumbled. 'I saw my sister Ally.'

'You were dreaming,' the voice insisted.

'No,' Ken said, shaking his head from side to side. Static electricity ran blue and white through his hair. 'No. I saw her. She's close and she's in trouble.'

'A dream. Nothing more than a dream.'

The voice faded and Ken slipped into a deep and dreamless sleep.

The hand that gripped the edge of the stone was more beast's paw than human hand. Coarse black hair sprouted on the back of the hand and the nails had curled long and black.

With a huge effort, Blade heaved himself over the top of the wall and lay gasping on the ground. The climb up the outside of Baddalaur's wall had exhausted him and on more than one occasion he had lost his precarious foot or handhold and dangled in mid-air, while he desperately scrabbled for a hole or niche in the wall. The climb had been made even more difficult because the were-change had begun working its way through his body while he'd been on the wall, brought on by the exhausting effort of climbing. He'd been forced to stop twice as his heart pounded crazily, until he felt as if it was going to burst from his chest.

Now, lying on his back, staring up at the stars, Blade realised that Scathach hadn't been lying. He could feel the muscles in his thighs and back actually twisting and moving beneath his skin, and his scalp was itching madly as coarse grey and black hair pushed its way upwards. The assassin was also aware that his sight was worsening, all the colours were fading, he could no longer see details as clearly and everything was beginning to look flat. To balance the loss however, he realised that his hearing had improved tremendously and his sense of smell had been enhanced.

He was turning into a Torc Allta.

Blade looked up at the sky again, but he was no longer able to see the stars, only the very vaguest suggestions of light and shade in the heavens. How much time had he left ... and would he be able to get his message to someone before the beast spell took over and turned him into a were-boar?

Blade raised himself to his hands and feet. He tried to stand upright, but he discovered his back wouldn't straighten. He hadn't much time left.

He had climbed onto a gently sloping roof that was five storeys above the ground. He had chosen it because it was thrown into permanent shadow by the bulk of the rest of the college and its ceiling was of thatch. Blade pulled out his knife, but he couldn't hold it properly in his clumsy hand-paws and it fell, slithering off the straw to fall to the ground far below with a faint ping of metal. The assassin bared his teeth, then, drawing his paw back, he drove it into the straw, punching a hole through into the room below. Quickly widening the hole, Blade dropped into the room ... and prayed that it was empty.

He had landed in a storeroom, piled high with mouldering beds and musty blankets. His sensitive hearing could distinguish the sounds of rats and mice moving through the straw mattresses. Crossing to the door, he cracked it open and peered out. The corridor outside was in darkness, but he found his beast-sight allowed him to distinguish features — the doors on either side of the corridor and the stairway at the far end.

Scuttling on all fours the beast-man darted down the long narrow corridor, keeping to the shadows. At the top of the stairs he stopped, nose wrinkling, trying to sort through the hundreds of new scents that he was now aware of. He smelt food and stale clothes, burning wood, the musty odour of old books ... and faint, very faint, the metallic odour of magic. Raising his head, Blade drew in a deep lungful of air, trying to trace the scent. It was coming from below, and it was mingling with the rich odour of soil and warm stone. Blade waited until a shuddering spasm had rippled through him, stretching his clothes to breaking point, misshapen feet now bursting through his boots, before he set off down the stairs, claws clicking off the smooth stones.

Colum, the Earthlord, rested his small hands on the stone and nodded his head. 'Here. Definitely here.' He turned around, and the bards and scholars crowding close to him, moved back, awed by the magical power that shimmered around his tiny body, dancing in green and brown lines of energy through his hair and across his skin.

Two of the bards were holding up an ancient wrinkled plan of the college. Colum pointed to a narrow corridor drawn in yellow ink that seemed to run deep below Baddalaur's thick walls. 'This corridor lies behind this wall. It runs out beneath the college and ends up on an island in the marshlands.'

The bards nodded. Everyone knew that a twisting network of tunnels honeycombed the ancient building. However, only a few of the tunnels were known; over the years many had collapsed, others had been forgotten, or the secret mechanisms used to open and close the doors had rusted solid, making them useless. For the past few days however, all the bards and scholars had turned their attentions to tracing the network of tunnels, and in particular one tunnel which was said to run out of the college and into the safety of the marshes. In the ancient past, when Baddalaur had been a fortress, the bards had used this tunnel to carry messages to the outside world, or to bring in supplies. It was one of the reasons the college had never been captured. However, in those days, the college had had an army of its own to protect it. But now there was no army, and everyone knew that they could not withstand a sustained assault by Scathach and her vampir army.

Although the bards had discovered the tunnel on the chart, they had been unable to find its entrance. Colum had sat down with a chart of the college before him and, using his earthmagic, he had traced the lines of soil and rock, feeling for imperfections and wounds in the ground. Then he had traced all those channels back to their source, until he had discovered the lost tunnel in a small cellar far below Baddalaur.

One of the bards came and knelt by the wall and ran his hand over its dusty surface. 'This is the oldest part of the college,' he muttered, 'all the walls are as thick as the length of my arm. We'll need digging tools, and even if we do break through, there's no guarantee that the tunnel will still be intact. It could have collapsed.' He shook his head wearily. 'I'm not sure if we have the time to excavate it ... in fact, I'm not sure if we even have the time to break through this stone.'

The small dark-skinned boy gently eased the man to one side. Then, placing both hands on the slab of stone, he lowered his head and closed his eyes. Everyone in the room felt the surge of magic that filled the chamber, soaking up through their feet as the earth itself fuelled the boy's powers.

And the stone melted.

One moment it was a piece of solid granite, the next bubbles had appeared on its surface, they burst, long liquid curls of stone dribbling onto the floor where they were absorbed into the earth. In less than twenty heartbeats the granite block had simply ceased to exist, leaving a gaping hole behind it. Cold, damp air flooded the room.

Colum put his head into the opening, nostrils flaring, brown eyes wide and staring, but he wasn't peering into the darkness, instead he saw the seams and strata of rocks and soil all around him. 'There is a rockfall about a hundred paces into the tunnel. It's not deep; we should be able to dig through it easily enough. There's a lot of mud and silt in the tunnel, but other than that it seems clean until it reaches the marshes.' He pulled his head out of the tunnel. 'If you put some men to clearing it, we can start evacuating the people in the morning.'

One of the older bards shook his head. 'I'm still not convinced that it is necessary to evacuate the college. I'm inclined to think that Scathach won't attack us; she knows our reputations, knows we have no army to send against her. I think we should stay here and sit it out.'

'Scathach will attack,' Colum said simply, 'and if she does, there is very little I can do to defend us. When Balor forced me to use my powers to destroy his enemies, he meddled with the very forces which hold this island together, weakening the links of stone and soil. Already, deep below the ground, in the heart of the earth, the molten rock is shifting and moving, the great plates of stone are tilting. If I am forced to use another great burst of power, I could unleash the raw elemental earthmagic ... and it would rip this island apart.'

'You won't have to use your earthmagic,' the old bard said firmly. 'Scathach won't attack.'

'*The Baobhan Sith will attack tonight.*'

The voice was a rasping growl. Claws slithered and clicked off the stone and then a creature — more boar than man — heaved its way into the cellar.

'The Baobhan Sith will attack tonight. Scathach has sworn to burn the library to the ground and turn everyone to vampir. Help me ... please.' Blade collapsed onto the ground.

Colum knelt by the creature's side, stretching out his hand to touch the furred skin, but drawing it back when he felt the tingle of magic. 'What ... who are you?'

'I am Blade.'

Some of the bards moved back, others drew their knives.

'Ragallach's bite,' Colum murmured. He lifted the creature's hand, moving it into the light. It had completely altered and twisted into a boar's hoof.

'It's a trap,' a bard hissed. 'Kill the thing now!'

'Scathach told me she could control the were-spell, but I threw away the protective collar to come here and warn you. She intends to destroy Baddalaur, to raze it to the ground.' The remains of Blade's single hand closed about the Earthlord's arm. 'You have to stop her. She intends to conquer the entire island ... and then the world.'

Colum nodded. 'Why did you come here?'

'To warn you.' He held up his injured hand. 'To ask for your help.'

Colum straightened and looked up into the troubled faces of the scholars and bards. 'We can't leave,' he said simply. 'We have to stay and protect the library.'

'We're scholars, teachers, historians, bards: we can't fight.'

'You have no choice!' Colum snapped. 'If you don't, then Scathach will destroy everything you and the previous generations have built. She will plunge this world into an age of darkness!'

The Earthlord stopped as a solemn bell began tolling, the peals vibrating through the stones.

'The College bell,' the old bard whispered, 'it hasn't been rung for centuries.'

'Scathach has come!' Blade gurgled.

Blade had betrayed her.

When she realised that he had vanished she sent search parties to comb the town of Baddalaur. They hadn't discovered Blade, but they had found the shattered remnants of his metal and stone collar. Closing her fist around the remains of the magical amulet, she crushed the stone to dust and crumpled the metal, realising that he had gone to betray her plans to the bards. It didn't matter now: by morning, the were-change would have altered him forever. But it did change her plans. Blade had been going to lead a small raiding party into the college by a route known only to himself. So now they had lost the element of surprise and because there was no-one else to lead her vampir, she would have to do it herself. But the more time she spent here, the more time it gave the other cities to learn of her existence and make preparations.

Baddalaur must fall quickly.

The Grey Warrior strode out of the darkened room she had made her headquarters and glared at the enormous tower of Baddalaur. She had been going to send fifty men in with Blade. Fifty should have been enough. But why send fifty when she could send fifty times fifty? The Baobhan Sith's pointed teeth flashed white in a triumphant smile. She would pit her entire vampir army against the college.

The captured bards and scholars would swell her army ... and the flames of Baddalaur would light her on her way.

As the sun rose over the De Danann Isles, it reached the Fomor Isles first, touching the tops of the cliffs, bringing the birds to screaming life, then moving downwards to wash, in light and shadow, the carvings set into the cliff-faces before bathing the wine groves in the pale sunshine.

The chill morning sunlight also washed over the long stream of nathair that rose in perfect unison out of the Fomor caves.

Two hundred black war-nathair, bred for strength and speed, flapped their translucent wings and flew low across the island. The highly skilled riders manipulated the nathair's hoods so that the serpents couldn't see the confusing sparkle as they crossed the short stretch of water separating the island from the Forest of Caesir.

In the safety of the trees, the Gor Allta and the Simpan-sai watched the exodus in alarm and wondered what disaster was about to befall the De Danann Isle.

Leading the nathair column, Morc twisted around in the high saddle to look behind him. His ragged teeth flashed in a smile. It had been too long since he had led the Fomor to battle — and it felt good!

Behind him, Cichal also smiled, but he was simply grinning at the thought of riding to the aid of the human-kind. Yesterday, such an idea would have been inconceivable. But the human whelps had changed that, three humans with the courage to carry their plea into the heart of the Fomor island. If the circumstances had been reversed, he wondered if one of the Fomor would have been brave enough to beg the human Emperor for help. Probably not, he had to admit, unless he was an exceptional Fomor. As he glanced over his shoulder at the three humans, he realised that they were indeed, exceptional people.

On the back of the third nathair, sandwiched between Faolan and Paedur, Megan shivered in the icy breeze. 'How long will it take us to get there?' she asked, the wind whipping her voice away.

'We should reach Baddalaur around noon,' Faolan called back.

'Let's hope we're not too late,' she said.

'We'll be in plenty of time,' Paedur assured her with a confidence that he did not feel.

~

As the sun rose higher in the heavens, its wan yellow light washed across Baddalaur's walls and illuminated the town beneath the ancient college. Shapes scuttled from the clean sunlight and retreated into the shadows, leaving a single grey-haired grey-clad warrior in the middle of the street.

Scathach was almost speechless with rage. Her first attack on the college had failed.

The Grey Warrior had expected a quick victory. But when she had reached the thick, metal-studded gates, she discovered that they were all locked and that heavy metal grids had been lowered in place, both before and behind the gates. As her vampir army neared, a deep bell had suddenly boomed out from within the college, and abruptly the high walls had bristled with armed men. Stones, spears, knives and arrows began raining down on her vampir, the shock of the blows rendering many of them unconscious.

Scathach had howled aloud her rage as she watched her vampir being pushed back. This was all Blade's fault. He knew all the secret ways into the college. If he had been with her, this would never have happened. When she found him, she was going to make him wish he had never been born. She would teach him that there were worse things than the were-curse.

When she realised that she wasn't going to take the college by stealth, she had called off her army and sent them into the shadows while she formulated another plan.

Now, standing in the street, watching the sunrise move across the walls, turrets and towers of the college, the Grey Warrior closed her eyes and began calling all the vampir to her. When they had assembled, she would surround Baddalaur and unleash her army on it from all sides at once. The plan would work: the defenders would never be able to withstand the combined assault of five thousand people ... and the human-kind wouldn't be expecting the vampir to attack during the day.

~

Ken could feel the sunbeams before he woke. He was aware of the flow of energy into his body as he absorbed the heat, felt the ancient power that trembled through his body, setting his muscles twitching, his nerves jangling. Rising up off the stone bed, he walked to the window and breathed in the cool morning air. He felt ... *alive*.

Alive and powerful. So powerful.

Stretching out his right hand, he watched as a miniature sun formed in the palm, the ball of light twisting and spinning, throwing off streamers of fire. Closing his hand on the ball, he felt the flames absorbed into his skin like cool water.

'You're awake at last.'

Ken turned as Foltor came into the room. The priest was carrying a wooden beaker of water and a deep bowl of gruel.

'How do you feel?' the priest asked.

'I feel ... good.' Ken nodded quickly, suddenly realising that he had never felt this well before. 'I feel alive.'

'The power of fire is working its magic within you,' Foltor continued. 'It will destroy any diseases or imperfections within you, strengthen your muscles, make you physically powerful. In time, you will also discover that you possess other gifts.' He stood beside Ken, his wrinkled face expressionless. 'Look at the sun,' he said, 'tell me what you see.'

'I can't look directly at the sun; it could blind me,' the boy protested.

'The sun is fire and you are fire. Look,' the old man insisted.

Ken turned his face to the east, staring deep into the sun. For a moment, he could see nothing but the blinding disc. His eyes watered. Brushing a hand across his eyes, he suddenly realised that he could see the shape of the sun clearly. It seemed close enough to reach out and touch. He watched as dark spots appeared and disappeared on its surface and he was actually able to see long streamers of fire shoot upwards from the heart of the sun.

'Now look down into the earth,' Foltor commanded, his voice echoing as if from a great distance.

Ken lowered his gaze, staring hard at the desert sands. The image of the sun danced on his eyes, colours and lines of light shimmering on the golden grains of sand. He blinked hard, squeezing his eyes shut, and when he opened them again, he discovered that the desert sands had been replaced by a molten pit of lava. Huge globules of burning rock twisted and turned in the heart of the fire, great slabs of stone cracking and snapping.

'You have looked into the heart of the sun, now you are seeing the heart of the earth.' Foltor's voice was distant, echoing softly inside the boy's head. 'The Earthlord's magic has weakened the bonds which hold this island together. All across the island, the fire-mountains have awoken, the earth trembles regularly, great chasms have opened up, rivers have sprouted where none had flowed before, others have soaked back into the earth, islands have risen in the seas. And all because the fires in the earth are in turmoil. If they are not calmed, then they will burst up and destroy this island.

'You wondered why you were brought here. The Goddess Danu sent you to us, so that we could train you in the Firelore. Only you can control and tame the fires. That is your destiny: to save the De Danann Isle from total destruction!'

Ken staggered back, deliberately looking away from the desert. For a moment the room swayed around him and Foltor gripped his arm for support. 'I can't ...' he began.

'You can,' the priest said firmly. 'You must.'

'I need more training,' Ken insisted.

Doubt flickered behind Foltor's eyes, and the boy knew that the priest agreed. 'There is no more time. Already events are moving to a conclusion. Scathach has besieged Baddalaur with her vampir army. She intends to destroy the building and the bards. If she succeeds she will set back the history of this world by many thousands of years. Learning builds upon learning, and if she ruins the library, there will be no new inventions, no discoveries, no advancement.'

'I could stop her!' Ken said excitedly. 'I could use my fire against her army.'

'And annihilate many thousands of innocent people? Their only crime is that they are controlled by Scathach. No, that is not your task,' Foltor said firmly. 'Paedur, Faolan and Megan have roused the Fomor to the defence of human-kind. Let them do battle with the vampir. Your task is to work with the Earthlord to mend the damage his magic has wrought. On no account must he be allowed to use his powers again before you repair the rifts in the earth's core.'

'You mentioned Paedur, Faolan, Megan and Colum,' Ken said, 'but what about Ally and Ragallach? Where is my sister?'

'We do not know.'

'Can you find her?'

'She is your sister,' Foltor said quickly, 'you can find her.'

'How?' Ken demanded.

'Use your magic. See her in your mind's eye, concentrate on her, call her.'

Closing his eyes, Ken concentrated on Ally's face, seeing her bright green eyes, her flame-red hair clearly. The colour of her hair suddenly fascinated him, it wasn't simply red, it was gold and bronze and brown, the colour of fire ...

'*Ally*,' he murmured.

Ally was dreaming of home, of a warm bed in her own room, with the familiar posters on the wall, all the cupboard doors open, books piled on the shelves, clothes scattered all over the floor. She was warm and snug ... until someone called her name and turned on the light.

She came awake with the sun in her face. In the single heartbeat it took for the memories to come flooding back — she was on the De Danann Isle, lost in the desert — she realised that Ragallach was gone. She leaned forward ... and suddenly remembered that she was sitting in a tree. With a short scream, she fell out of the tree and crashed to the ground below. Sand billowed and settled over her.

Rolling over, groaning as her bruised back and shoulders protested, she opened her eyes. Ragallach was above her, paw outstretched to help her to her feet. 'Are you all right?' he asked anxiously.

'I didn't know sand could be so hard,' she muttered. 'I'd forgotten I was in the tree,' she admitted sheepishly.

'I'm sorry. I was going to tie a belt around you, but I didn't want to wake you. I was sure I'd be back before you woke up. I was hunting for breakfast,' he added, opening his paws to reveal three black-skinned fruits.

'Breakfast?' Ally prodded one of the fruits with her finger. The skin was surprisingly soft and her nail punctured the surface;

clear sticky liquid oozed out. 'Looks like an avocado,' she muttered. 'What are they?'

'I don't know,' Ragallach said, 'but the birds were eating them, so they're safe to eat.' Handing one to Ally, he popped another into his enormous mouth and began chewing, his jaws moving from side to side. Then he swallowed hard. 'It's disgusting.'

'I think you should have taken the peel off first,' the girl laughed, having cracked the fruit in half and nibbled at the interior. It was sharp and sweet, the pale green interior looking and tasting a little like kiwi-fruit.

They walked down to the water's edge, their sudden appearance sending dozens of small sparkling lizards scuttling for cover. A snake twisted and curled its way across the sands, leaving a trail of S's across the footprints of the other creatures.

Ally knelt by the water's edge and peered in. The water was so clear, she could see right to the bottom. 'Is this safe to drink?' she wondered aloud.

Ragallach, who was busy digging out the insides of the last of the fruits, raised his head and his flattened nostrils twitched. 'Probably,' he grunted. 'But I wouldn't,' he added as Ally scooped up a handful of water. She allowed it to trickle from between her fingers. 'I could probably drink it and suffer no ill-effects, but you human-kind are weaker, your stomachs not so robust. The water could make you very ill.'

'It looks clear,' Ally muttered, scooping up another handful of water and staring closely at it.

'My nose tells me that this is the only water around here for at least a day's journey. That means that every bird, beast and insect uses it for drinking, washing and ... everything else!'

Ally allowed the water to fall back into the pool and rubbed her hand in her trousers. 'I'm thirsty,' she said softly.

'I could get some more fruit,' Ragallach said, 'the juice isn't so bad.'

Ally sank to the ground in the soft margin beside the pool. 'What are we going to do Ragallach?' she sighed.

The Torc Allta sat beside her, dipping his bare feet into the water, and began shaping the mud into soft balls. 'I can't deny we are in serious trouble,' he admitted, taking one of the balls and rubbing it onto Ally's forehead. She closed her eyes and allowed the damp mud to soothe her sunburn. 'I've been thinking. We have two choices: we can stay here ... or we can move on.'

'That's not much of a choice.'

'If we stay here,' Ragallach said, ignoring the interruption, 'the others will come and look for us.'

'Eventually,' Ally added.

'Eventually,' Ragallach agreed. 'But I'm not sure we could both survive until then. There is some fruit certainly, but not enough for two. And we've no way of cleaning the water.'

Ally tilted her chin upwards as Ragallach smeared mud on her cheeks and ears. 'What's our other choice?'

'One of us could strike out for the nearest civilisation,' the Torc Allta said softly, 'while the other remains here. There's enough fruit for one.'

Ally opened her eyes. 'One of us?' she asked. She picked up a mudball and stuck it on Ragallach's forehead with enough force to make the Torc Allta blink. 'Which one?'

'Me of course. It makes sense,' he grunted. 'You stay here, live off the fruits. I'll head for the Cliffs of Laghairt Dis.'

'How far is that?'

Ragallach shrugged. 'Three days by foot, maybe four.'

'A three or four day journey,' Ally snapped angrily, 'with no food and no water. You'd never make it.'

'I am a Torc Allta. I can survive for a long time with no food and little water.'

The girl slapped on more mud and began smearing it around the were-creature's small pink eyes. 'And what happens at night when you return to your pig form? You were asleep last night, you didn't hear the zoo that gathered down here around the pool to eat and drink and kill each other.'

'I could burrow into the sands.'

'What about snakes ... and lizards ... and those flying nathair-things?' she snapped.

Ragallach caught hold of Ally's hands and held them tightly. 'Why are you fighting with me?'

'I'm not!'

'You are. We don't have any other choice, Ally,' he reminded her. 'You stay here; I'll go for help. I'll be back in a couple of days. It makes sense.'

Ally pulled away from the Torc Allta and turned her back on him. Folding her arms across her chest, she walked away from the pool and stood staring out through the trees at the shimmering sands. 'I'm not fighting with you,' she said very quietly. 'I'm fighting with me. This is all my fault.'

Ragallach stood up and put his hands on her shoulders. 'No, it's not.'

'It is. You're only here because you came with me ...'

'I made my own decision,' Ragallach said firmly. 'That's what life is all about: making decisions. I chose to come with you.'

'But you didn't have to.'

'I wanted to. You would have done the same for me, wouldn't you?'

'Yes,' she said without hesitation.

'That's what friends do,' Ragallach said simply, 'and we are friends, aren't we?'

Ally turned to look at Ragallach. She nodded very slowly, suddenly wondering why her eyes were full of tears. 'Yes, we are friends.'

Ragallach opened his mouth to speak, then his head suddenly snapped around, eyes wide and staring, moist nostrils flaring.

'Rag ...' Ally began.

The Torc Allta suddenly caught her shoulders with bruising force and sent her sailing through the air into the middle of the pool. Her scream of rage and shock was drowned by a mouthful of brackish water. Rising, spluttering from the pool, she was in time to see an enormous lion-like creature step through the undergrowth and approach Ragallach. Two enormous fang-like teeth jutted from its upper jaw.

'Stay in the water!' Ragallach squealed, moving in the other direction, leading the sabre-tooth away from the girl.

And then the lion lowered itself onto its belly and launched itself at the Torc Allta.

Ally screamed.

Her hair was the colour of copper, with solid threads of pure gold woven through it.

Ken suddenly realised that he could see his sister. He blinked: he could see her clearly — she was in the middle of a pool of foaming water, her mouth wide, eyes horrified.

'*Ally*,' he whispered, using her name to help him concentrate on her. '*Ally*.'

The scene tilted and shifted, dropping away from him, and it was as if he was flying high over the desert, moving effortlessly through space. The desert spread as far as he could see, brown and gold and ochre, but directly below him was the green and sparkling silver of an oasis.

'*Ally*,' he called again. '*Ally*.'

He fell, pulled down to earth, the oasis zooming up with terrifying speed until he could make out the individual trees around the circular pool. There was something red in the pool. And at the side of the pool a long sabre-tooth lion was locked in a savage battle with a boar.

It took a moment for the images Ken was seeing to make sense, and then he too screamed aloud his rage and fear.

~

Ragallach had been trying to lead the beast away from the pool and Ally when it pounced, its weight driving him to the ground, its warm, moist breath foul on his face. He struck it hard on the nose, and it shook its head, enormous teeth slicing through the air before his face. Ragallach managed to roll out from beneath it and run a dozen steps before it brought him down again.

~

Ally saw the lion land on Ragallach's back and drive him forwards and down into the bushes. She screamed aloud his name, but her cry was drowned in the savage growling of the beast.

And then the lion's triumphant roars were lost beneath the deafening peal of thunder directly overhead. The air turned cold, stinking of burnt metal and then with a crack, a solid spear of fire lanced from the sky and stabbed into the bushes, crisping them to ashes. The lion's roars abruptly silenced.

'*Ally.*'

The girl distinctly heard her brother's voice.

'*Ally. I'm coming, Ally.*'

But Ally ignored the sounds in her head. Sick with fear, she dragged herself from the pool and crept closer to the cindered bushes. 'Ragallach?' she called.

But there was no reply.

From a window in Baddalaur's highest tower, Colum looked down over the college and the surrounding town. Blade crouched by his side. The bards had used a spell, similar to Scathach's, to prevent the were-spell from completely claiming his body, but they had been unable to reverse the changes which had worked their way through him. Now he was caught in a terrifying misshapen mixture of man and beast, neither human nor Torc Allta, but something in between.

Colum leaned on the windowledge and stared down. From this great height it looked as if the college building was· surrounded by thousands of ants, all moving and turning in unison. Then, on an unheard command, the tiny figures turned towards the college.

'It begins,' the Earthlord whispered. 'I didn't realise that there were that many people in the town.'

'Scathach told me she commanded an army of five thousand,' Blade growled. 'It is obvious she has unleashed them all on Baddalaur. She is determined to destroy this place.'

'But they are vampir; they are creatures of the night, they should not be able to move about during the day,' Colum protested.

'Scathach is Baobhan Sith; she can make the vampir do anything she wants them to. Eventually however, the heat and light of the sun will burn and blister their skins. If they remain in the light too long then they will go blind.'

'But they're innocent people!' Colum protested.

'Scathach doesn't care.'

'I've got to stop her.'

'How?' Blade growled.

The boy took a deep breath, then his shoulders slumped. 'I don't know,' he admitted.

~

The vampir launched themselves against Baddalaur's walls with increasing ferocity. They pounded at the gates with every weapon and tool they could lay their hands on, and when the tools broke, they used their fists. They hurled stones and spears, fired slingshots and arrows at the defenders, and although many of their shots fell far short of the target, a few struck home, sending a scholar or bard reeling back off the balcony.

More of the vampir started to dig in beneath the walls, using shovels and spades, and bare hands to gouge out a deep hole to get at the foundations. Others attempted to set fire to the studded wooden doors, dousing them in fish-oil before setting them alight. And on all sides the vampir pushed crude ladders up against the walls.

The few defenders were stretched thin, running from place to place, pushing off the ladders, pouring oil and boiling water onto the attackers below, dropping stones, firing bows and crossbows and spears into the vampir.

But there were too few defenders, and they found it difficult to fire on people they had known all their lives: friends, neighbours, relatives. And even when the vampir were knocked down with spear or knife or sword, they just got up and marched on, their faces expressionless.

But what terrified the defenders even more was that the attack was conducted in complete silence. The vampir didn't scream or shout or cry aloud. They moved like sleepwalkers, arms outstretched, eyes blank and unseeing, mouths gaping to reveal pointed teeth.

And the defenders knew that it was only a matter of time before the walls were breached and Baddalaur fell.

~

In the pitch-black of a musty cellar, Scathach crouched, eyes squeezed tightly shut, mouth locked in a grim line, sweat gleaming on her pale face. The effort of controlling the vampir army was exhausting. It had been a mistake to send so many against Baddalaur, she knew that now. However, it was too late to draw back. The Baobhan Sith was aware of every individual vampir, conscious that while some were easy to control and took no effort, others fought against the vampir spell, perhaps realising that her control was slipping. She would have to win soon or she would lose control of the vampir.

She watched through the eyes of some of her vampir, as the ancient wooden gates of Baddalaur finally burst into flame, billowing dark greasy smoke high into the skies.

She saw some of her vampir crack open a huge stone close to the foot of the walls.

She waited while ladder after ladder was placed against the walls. The defenders managed to push them all back, but to do so they had to expose themselves, and one by one they were falling beneath the rain of arrows of spears. Shortly there would be no-one left to push the ladders away.

~

'You must use your power. You are our only hope.'

Colum looked at the faces of the few assembled bards. The elders of the college had gathered in the hall of the Great Library in a desperate attempt to prepare a plan to defend Baddalaur.

'More than half of our men are wounded; others have simply refused to fight because they cannot face the thought of injuring a relative or friend. You must help us!'

The boy shook his head. 'I cannot. You know that. If I use any of my power, it could set in motion a train of events that would destroy the island.'

'But there must be something you can do?' an elderly bard demanded. 'Make the earth shake, open up pits ...'

There was a sudden grating crash, followed by a long slow groaning as stones crashed down. In the silence that followed, the shouts of the defenders were clearly audible.

'*The walls*!'

'*The walls are breached*!'

And then another cry was taken up, high-pitched and strident.

'*Fomor*!'

'*Fomor are coming.*'

~

In a long snaking line, the war nathair spread out, one group following Morc wheeling around to the left, the other forming behind Cichal and heading to the right, encircling the town and the college.

For a single instant there was a lull in the battle — and then the Fomor sent their huge beasts crashing into the attackers, driving them back in scattered confusion.

The air was filled with the stench of nathair and Fomor, the screams of the beasts and the cheers of the defenders. But above it all the voice of Morc was clearly audible.

'Baobhan Sith! I am coming for you, Baobhan Sith.'

~

The shock of the Fomor's arrival left Scathach stunned. She had been concentrating so hard on controlling the vampir that she hadn't even been aware of their approach.

Looking through the eyes of her vampir army, she saw the skies filled with black war-nathair. She spotted Cichal wielding his huge stone sword as he urged his nathair downwards, and there was Morc, the Fomor king, on another nathair waving a huge bone-handled battle axe.

Why were they here? As friends or foes?

Then she saw the figures on the back of another nathair — and Scathach's teeth bared in a savage grimace. The bard. The warrior-maid. The Windlord.

Even before the nathair crashed into her vampir and the Fomor leapt down, wielding swords and axes and battle-hammers, she knew why they had come.

And then she heard Morc's raised voice.

'Baobhan Sith. I am coming for you, Baobhan Sith.'

In that instant her concentration lapsed — and the entire vampir army slumped unconscious onto the ground.

Scathach staggered to her feet and climbed the steps out of the cellar, blinking in the brilliant mid-morning sunshine. Complete silence greeted her appearance, the Fomor warriors standing confused amongst the sleeping vampir, Baddalaur's defenders equally bewildered by the sudden turn of events.

Morc and Cichal appeared around the corner of a building, followed by Paedur, Megan and Faolan.

'It's over, Scathach,' Paedur called. 'You've lost.'

The Baobhan Sith hissed like a serpent, showing her pointed teeth. 'No bard, it's not finished yet.'

Morc stepped forward, hefting his battle axe. 'It is!'

Scathach threw back her head and laughed. Then, raising her hands high, she screamed aloud, 'Hiisi, Lord of Evil, Kalma, Goddess of Death, Tuomi, God of the Underworld, come to me now. Aid me! Aid me!'

'The vampir gods!' Paedur shouted, 'she's conjuring the vampir gods!'

Morc raced forward, raising his axe, but it was too late ...

Rua brought the nathair in low over the oasis, the wind from the serpent's wings sending sand swirling upwards from the dunes, its sudden appearance driving startled birds high into the air. Ken, who had been clinging tightly to the priest during the short flight from the hive, threw himself off the creature even before it had stopped and dropped to the ground, slithering down the side of a sand dune.

'Ally? Ally, where are you?'

There was no reply.

'Ally!'

Taking a deep breath, Ken calmed himself, trying to recall the last images he had seen of his sister. She had been in the water, just here, while the sabre-toothed lion had attacked Ragallach ... over there. The sight of the lion attacking the Torc Allta had sent a burst of rage through Ken and before he knew what had happened, a solid spear of fire had shot from the heavens and incinerated the lion. But the flash of light had blinded him, leaving him unable to see anything else. Foltor hadn't wanted him to leave, but the look in Ken's eyes and the crackles of raw magic that sparked from him with every move, convinced the priest that he couldn't keep the boy. Summoning Rua, the priest who had first encountered Ken, they had saddled one of the hive's few nathair and set off across the desert for the nearest oasis.

'Ally?'

Stepping closer to the pool, Ken looked around and immediately spotted the burnt and blackened remains of the bushes where lightning had struck the lion.

But there was no sign of Ally or Ragallach.

And then he spotted the footprints in the sand — small booted feet running from the pool towards the burnt bushes. Taking a deep breath, dreading what he was going to find, Ken followed them.

~

'Ally?'

Crouched on the blackened ground, the girl ignored the voice in her head.

'Ally?'

Ragallach was gone and it was all her fault. He had deliberately led the lion away from her, having thrown her to safety.

'Ally?'

When the lightning bolt struck the lion, she had raced from the pool, expecting to find ... she didn't know what she had been expecting to find.

She had found nothing.

'Ally?'

The ground was speckled red and brown with blood, but she didn't know whose. The sand where the thunderbolt struck had hardened to glass. But there was no sign of Ragallach, no sign of the lion. Sinking to the ground, she pressed her hands to the warm earth and wept bitterly for her lost friend.

'Ally?'

A hand touched her shoulder, and she screamed in fear and fright. When she looked up, she screamed again ... because she was looking at Ken.

A ghost. A mirage.

'Ally,' Ken breathed, 'you're all right.' Tears sparkled in his eyes.

Scrambling to her feet, Ally stretched out her hand and

touched Ken's cheek with the tips of her fingers. She touched warm flesh. 'You're real,' she whispered.

'I'm real,' he smiled.

'I was coming to look for you. Ragallach and me ...' She stopped, swallowing hard. 'And then we lost our nathair and ... and ...'

Ken wrapped his arms around his sister's shoulders and hugged her close. 'I know,' he whispered, rubbing her hair, 'I know.'

'There was a lion, a sabre-toothed lion ...'

'I know,' Ken said again.

'No, you don't!' Ally snapped, pulling back. 'You can't know. Ragallach lured it away from me. But it caught him ...' Her voice broke and she started sobbing. 'You can't know.'

'I do,' Ken whispered, blinking away tears. He couldn't tell his sister what he had seen in those last instants before the thunderbolt struck. 'I saw it all. I sent the thunderbolt.'

Ally looked at him blankly.

'I am the Firelord, Ally.'

'Firelord,' the girl breathed. She turned to look at the burnt bushes, the hardened ground. 'You sent the lightning? But what about Ragallach ..?' she asked.

'Gone,' Ken said simply.

'No, never gone.' Brother and sister turned as Rua appeared behind them, hands folded into the sleeves of his robe. 'While you remember him, he will live forever. That is the real nature of immortality.' The priest looked from Ken to Ally. 'He gave his life for you, you have a duty now to remember him. Will you remember him?'

'Always,' they said together.

'Then say his name,' Rua said.

'Ragallach na Torc Allta,' Ken said.

'My friend,' Ally murmured.

Walking back through the oasis, past the churned-up pool, Rua turned to Ally. 'How did you become stranded here?'

'We flew in on a nathair. But it was attacked by creatures Ragallach called Flying Devils. They looked like pterodactyls,' she added, looking at her brother.

'They were,' he said decisively. He reached inside the neck of his shirt and pulled out a long curled bone which he wore on a thong around his neck. 'This is a tooth — I think from a Tyrannosaurus Rex.'

Ally reached for the bone — and a spark of cold blue fire snapped from Ken's fingertips and curled around her hand. 'It's the firelore,' he apologised. 'I still can't fully control it. When I saw the sabre-tooth attacking Ragallach and threatening you, I just felt so angry ... and then my rage boiled up and flowed out of me in a solid stream of fire.'

'What happened to Ragallach?' Ally asked suddenly.

Ken looked at her blankly.

'Did your ... magic destroy him?'

Ken opened his mouth to reply, but he couldn't think of an answer. It was also a question he had been asking himself.

'No,' Rua said, surprising them both. 'Ragallach was Torc Allta. One of the Clan Allta, a shape-shifter. When one of the Clan Allta dies, they leave no physical body behind. Scholars have argued about this, and believe it is because the shape-shifter's body is in a constant state of change and alteration. Death for them is just another alteration. At the moment of death they simply ... vanish.'

They walked on in silence, then Ally glanced sidelong at her brother. He was a year younger than her, and had always been juvenile and awkward, but now he moved with a new sense of confidence and assurance.

'So you're really the Firelord?'

Ken nodded. 'I am,' he said proudly. 'The priests believe that this is the reason I was brought to the De Danann Isle in the first place.'

'How many Flying Devils attacked your nathair?' Rua asked suddenly, interrupting Ally's train of thought: why had she been brought to the isle?

'Two,' she said.

The bald priest quickened his pace. 'There must be a nest close by,' he muttered. 'The Flying Devils enjoy nathair meat,' he added. He started running. 'We must get away from here.'

As the trio burst out of the shelter of the trees, they stopped. The sky to the west was filled with thirty Flying Devils, some high in the sky, others flying low over the sands, huge shadows rippling across the dunes. They were all heading directly for the tethered nathair.

'No!' Ally stared at the approaching pterosaurs in horror. She felt a wave of despair wash over her: it was happening again. The pterosaurs would eat the nathair, leaving them trapped in the oasis, back where they started ... and Ragallach would have died for nothing. Maybe it would be better if the pterosaurs ate them too ...

'Firelord?' Rua made the single word into a question.

Ken stepped forward, the movement attracting the attention of the narrow-beaked birds. Mouths opened, revealing rows of triangular teeth. Ally went to follow him, but Rua pulled her back. 'Wait. Watch,' the priest said.

Ken scrambled up onto the top of a low sand dune and waved his arms in the air to attract the creatures' attention. The huge lizards wheeled in perfect precision and headed towards him, wings beating furiously, some of them so close to the ground that the sand curled and twisted in eddies and spirals around their bodies.

Ken spread his arms wide and tilted his face to the sun, eyes wide and staring.

The pterosaurs were closer now. Ally could see their dead crocodile eyes, the patina of scales — or was it feathers — on their breasts and bellies, the hundreds of teeth which filled their narrow beaks.

Ken brought his hands together with a clap ... and flames engulfed his hands.

Fireballs gathered around his hands, gloves of spinning, twisting spheres of flame. Drawing his right arm back he made a throwing motion at the nearest Flying Devil. A solid ball of flame shot from his hand and splashed against the pterosaur, bringing it crashing to the ground wrapped in streamers of fire. One of the pterosaurs broke off to land beside its stricken companion and peck at it with its savage beak.

The remainder of the pterosaurs surrounded the boy, diving and screaming, the air filled with their musty pungent odour. Ken ignored the creatures. Again and again, he drew back his hands, sending balls and streamers of fire into the midst of the pterosaurs. A dozen fell to the sands where they burned furiously, some, in a desperate attempt to avoid the flames, went crashing into others, and then the two birds started fighting, tearing at each other with teeth and claws. One, ignoring the Firelord, darted in towards Ally and Rua. It got within ten paces of them before an intense blue flame washed over it, charring it to a blackened skeleton in mid-air.

Thirty pterosaurs had flown to the oasis, drawn by the stink of nathair and human meat. Three escaped.

~

Rua caught Ken before he slumped to the ground, exhausted by the sudden release of magic.

'Is he all right?' Ally asked anxiously.

'He's fine. The fire magic has sapped his energy.' Rua eased Ken onto the dunes. 'Let him sleep in the sun for awhile. The light of Nusas will revive him.'

'What happens now?' Ally asked, suddenly feeling exhausted.

'Now we head to Baddalaur,' Rua said straightening, brushing his hand across his bald head. 'With Ken's control of the Firelore, and the Earthlord's magic, we can remake the land, calm the grumbling forces deep in the earth.' The man smiled quickly, stiffly, as if he wasn't used to smiling. 'You should be happy. You have helped save the De Danann Isle.'

'But at what cost ...?' Ally asked softly, looking back at the oasis, thinking of Ragallach. For an instant the air shimmered in the heart of the oasis, and she thought she saw a pair of tiny pink eyes regarding her above a savage tusked smile. She blinked and the image vanished.

'Hiisi, Lord of Evil, Kalma, Goddess of Death, Tuomi, God of the Underworld, come to me now. Aid me! Aid me!'

Hiisi appeared first. The creature coalesced out of thin air, a smoky shadowy shape that towered above Morc. The smoke hardened, and the creature took on a physical existence.

Hiisi was ancient and evil, the face a savage skull, bald with huge tusks protruding from its upper jaw, and deep sunk blazing red eyes. Its skin was the texture of stone, cracked and pitted and scored like old rock, and its finger length nails tapered to needle-sharp points.

The creature caught Morc's axe in mid-air, plucked it from his hand and snapped it in half. Then it slashed at Morc, and the ancient Fomor only escaped the razor-sharp claws by flinging himself backwards with all his strength.

Kalma materialised in a blast of foul air. Unlike the Lord of Evil, the vampir Goddess of Death was beautiful. Dressed in a flowing crimson robe, Kalma was tall and slender, pale skinned, red-lipped with deep-sunk black eyes and a flowing mane of raven hair that touched the ground behind her. Then she opened her mouth ... and revealed a row of savage teeth and a flickering serpent's tongue. She hissed like a nathair, and spat a tiny ball of green acid that burned into the ground at Cichal's feet.

The dust before Scathach grew agitated and then the ground bulged upwards and split as Tuomi, God of the Underworld appeared, scrabbling his way out of the pit. The ground then closed behind him, like a mouth snapping shut. The creature was short and incredibly powerful looking, with a barrel chest and long muscled arms that touched the ground when he moved. His features were flat and beast-like, with a thick bony ridge over his eyes and almost no chin, which made his fangs even more prominent. A crest of bone rose on the top of his skull then followed the line of his spine to appear as a stub of a tail.

Scathach was laughing hysterically. 'You thought you could defeat me with this army of Fomor? Think again. These are my gods. A thousand years and more ago, they granted me immortality, and I have served them faithfully ever since.' The Baobhan Sith spread her arms wide. 'I was doing all this for them. First I was going to conquer the world, then I was going to present it to them as a gift. They could have spent the rest of eternity feasting off the human-kind. But now you have forced me to call them before their time. It doesn't matter though,' she added. 'They are hungry. They are always hungry. And now it's time for them to feed!'

Tuomi suddenly leapt forward, reaching for Megan. The girl's lightning fast reflexes saved her, as she dropped to one side and rolled beneath the creature's grasp. Paedur slashed at it with his hook, but the metal sang off Tuomi's skin. The god's tail flickered, catching the bard in the knee with a sickening crack, sending him crashing to the ground.

Hiisi reached for Morc, but Cichal threw himself in front of his king, his stone sword clutched in both hands. He brought it around in a wide sweeping cut that should have sliced the god in two ... but the sword shattered against the god's granite-like skin.

Hiisi caught Cichal and pulled him forwards, savage jaws gaping. The Fomor used his tail to catch the god on the side of the head, the blow surprising it, and then Morc struck the god from behind with all his might, fragments of stone chipping away from Hiisi's skin. The god dropped Cichal, who was pulled away by Morc.

Kalma fixed on Faolan, her vampir's eyes burning redly with an inner fire. The Windlord stiffened, as if he had been struck and suddenly he took a step forward. The goddess hissed delightedly.

Megan caught Faolan's arm, and tried to drag him back, but the boy shook her off. Paedur, still lying on the ground, grabbed the Windlord's ankle, but Faolan kicked out, loosening the grip. 'Stop him,' Paedur shouted, attempting to come to his feet, but his injured knee gave way.

And then Megan threw herself onto Faolan's back and wrapped her hands in his golden hair and pulled. The excruciating pain suddenly brought the boy back to his senses.

Kalma spat, acid saliva searing into Faolan's forehead. He fell back screaming, eyes squeezed tightly shut, terrified that some of the venom would blind him. Megan dragged him away, wiping the green slime off with her fingers, ignoring the pain as it burnt her flesh. 'Use your magic,' she shouted.

'I can't,' he sobbed, 'I can't concentrate with the pain.'

'Back,' Morc shouted, 'fall back to the college.'

'Too late,' Paedur muttered, desperately trying to remember something that would help them.

'Kill them. Kill them all,' Scathach screamed.

The ancient and powerful vampir gods closed in on the three humans and the two Fomor.

~

On Baddalaur's walls, Colum closed his eyes and wept silently.

'No,' Blade grunted.

'I have to,' Colum said. Then he raised his hands.

~

The ground opened.

A crack, a tiny, eggshell crack appeared on the ground between the vampir gods and the humans and Fomor.

And then the earth shook. A tremble at first, then the shivering grew, intensified, and the crack widened, the earth snapping, cracking, breaking ... and then pulling apart.

'No, Colum,' Paedur screamed.

But it was too late.

One moment Scathach and the vampir gods were standing directly in front of Paedur and his companions ... the next they were separated by a gaping chasm. The sides of the pit crumbled away, rocks and chunks of earth tumbling into the river of lava that bubbled and spat far below.

~

On Baddalaur's walls, Colum slumped, exhausted by the effort of working the earthmagic. Blade nuzzled his hand. 'What have you done?' he grunted.

'I created a tiny rift in the earth and pushed it apart, separating Scathach and her gods from the others. I didn't use much power,' he whispered, 'not enough to upset the delicate balance in the interior of the earth.'

'Why is the earth still shaking then?' Blade asked.

Colum looked up, mouth and eyes widening in horror when he realised that the crack he had made was still growing, the lava rising, the earth still trembling.

~

The buildings behind Scathach went first, shuddering to the ground, before being swallowed by the pits which appeared all over Baddalaur. The ancient college building began to tremble, long cracks snaking up along the walls, battlements and the tops of towers swaying and then slowly toppling off to crash into the town below.

'To the nathair,' Cichal shouted. He caught Paedur and heaved him over his shoulder, while Megan led Faolan. 'Back. To the nathair!'

The earth split almost directly in front of him, fire spouting upwards, but the Fomor leapt over the crack.

Morc raced back towards his Fomor Troop. 'Take as many of the human-kind as you can carry. Flee south.'

Jagged lines were radiating through the town, sundering buildings, slicing through them as if they had been carved by a sword. Fires erupted in a dozen places. The taller buildings crashed to the ground, sloping tiled roofs sliding off, chimneys caving in through the roofs, whole sections of the streets disappearing into the cellars below, then the cellars themselves being swallowed up.

Then the earth tilted and shifted again — and the rift between Scathach and the others simply disappeared as the earth rejoined with a thunderous clap.

Howling with triumph, Scathach and her gods raced after the fleeing Fomor and humans.

~

'Run,' Morc hissed to Cichal, 'I'll hold them.'

'I'll stay.'

'Go. I command you,' the king snarled. 'The Fomor will need a strong leader.' Then he turned back to face the approaching vampir gods. In the last few heartbeats before they reached him, he found he was thinking of his son the Baobhan Sith had turned into a vampir. The burst of anger he felt lent him strength.

Hiisi, Lord of Evil, reached the Fomor king first, wrapping its taloned nails around his throat. From the corner of his eyes Morc saw Kalma and Tuomi continue after the others. The king struck the god, and then hissed aloud his pain. It was like striking granite; he felt as if he had shattered his claw. Hiisi ignored the blow and forced him back, driving him onto the ground, savage jaws gaping.

Slumped over Cichal's shoulder, Paedur was aware that Kalma, the Goddess of Death was closing fast. She spat at him, but her venom fell short and smoked on the ground.

And then the earth shook violently again, and Faolan stumbled and Megan fell and the two vampir gods were on top of them.

Tuomi snatched up Megan, her blows and kicks bouncing harm-
lessly off its thick skin, while Kalma fell onto Faolan, pinning
him to the ground, teeth bared, dripping venom.

Paedur's scream made Cichal turn, but he hesitated a moment
too long, torn between the two trapped human-kind and his king.

~

The fireball of intense blue-white flame washed across Kalma,
setting her hair alight ... a solid hammer of yellow fire drove
Tuomi backwards ... thin cords of white flame wrapped themselves around Hiisi and dragged him back off the Fomor king.

A dozen fireballs, spears of light and tiny flaming meteors of
burning rock struck the vampir gods, finger-sized drops of fire
rained down on them, driving them backwards, blinding them,
burning them. The ground beneath their feet popped alight as the
very earth curdled into molten lava, stones splitting with the
intensity of the heat, showering them with boiling splinters. The
gods turned and fled.

And the earth split wide open in a gaping wound.

Scathach, seeing what was about to happen, screamed a
warning, but her voice was swallowed in the maelstrom of sound.

Too late the gods realised that they were on the edge of a pit.
Tuomi managed to stop, but Hiisi and Kalma struck him, and the

three went over the edge together. When they eventually struck the bottom, disappearing into a bubbling pit of lava, the explosion sent a long streamer of flame high into the air.

Scathach raced to the edge of the pit, staring down, disbelievingly, unable to comprehend what had happened. A cracking sound made her look up, look around, afraid that the earth was breaking or a building about to tumble onto her. Her hand twitched and when she looked at it she discovered that the grey skin was deepening in colour, hardening, cracking, taking on the same texture as Hiisi's skin, that of old stone. There was a snap as her little finger simply fell off, shattering to dust when it touched the ground. Then her right hand began twitching, and the muscles in her legs spasmed.

She realised then what had happened. Her gods had died, and it was only her gods that had kept her alive all these many hundreds of years ...

Before she could scream, the Baobhan Sith's legs gave way, crumbling to dust, pitching her forwards, down into the pit to join her gods. Long before she reached the bottom she had turned to gritty stone dust.

~

The fires died as abruptly as they had started, and the earth stilled. And out of the swirling dust, a red-haired boy and girl appeared.

In the smoking ruins of the college of Baddalaur, the monks gathered the most important of their books and charts. They moved in absolute silence and with utmost caution, aware that the slightest sound could bring the entire building crashing down.

On the fields outside the college, the survivors of Scathach's vampir army were awakening one by one, lost and confused, convinced that they had just experienced a terrifyingly real nightmare.

On a low hill overlooking the ruined town, the six companions stood beside Morc and Cichal.

'I had to do it,' Colum said. 'I had to use my power. I couldn't allow you to be killed by those creatures.'

Paedur, leaning heavily on a stick, squeezed the Earthlord's shoulder. 'You did what you had to do.'

'What happens now?' Morc grunted. He turned to look at Ken. 'You are the new Firelord — can you control the fires in the earth?' As he was speaking, the earth trembled and shivered and another building in the town crashed down.

'For a little while,' Ken said slowly, 'but only for a little while, a few days at the most.'

'What happens then?' Megan asked.

Ken shook his head. 'I don't know.'

Colum looked up. 'Then the De Danann Isle will tear itself apart and sink beneath the waves in a day and a night. It's my fault,' he added.

'No,' Cichal said suddenly, 'there is no-one at fault here. Events and circumstances have led us to this place. We cannot look back; we must move on, look to the future.'

'What is the future?' Faolan asked bitterly. 'The De Danann Isle could sink beneath the waves at any moment.'

'Leave the island,' Ally said softly. Everyone turned to look at her. 'Gather together a fleet and set out for new lands. In my time,' she added, 'there is a legend about a powerful island empire that was destroyed by magic. But its people went out to bring knowledge and learning to the rest of the world.' She paused and then said firmly, 'That is your future: that is the destiny of the De Danann Isle.'